Anne Charlotte Leffler, Sofia Vasilevna Kovalevskaia

Sonia Kovalevsky

Biography and Autobiography

Anne Charlotte Leffler, Sofia Vasilevna Kovalevskaia

Sonia Kovalevsky
Biography and Autobiography

ISBN/EAN: 9783337064709

Printed in Europe, USA, Canada, Australia, Japan

Cover: Foto ©Raphael Reischuk / pixelio.de

More available books at **www.hansebooks.com**

SONIA KOVALEVSKY

Biography and Autobiography

I. *MEMOIR*

BY A. C. LEFFLER (EDGREN)

DUCHESSA DI CAJANELLO

II. *REMINISCENCES*
OF CHILDHOOD

WRITTEN BY HERSELF

Translated into English by

LOUISE VON COSSEL

LONDON: WALTER SCOTT, LTD.

PATERNOSTER SQUARE

1895

SONIA KOVALEVSKY

WHAT I KNOW ABOUT HER FROM
PERSONAL ACQUAINTANCE
AND WHAT SHE TOLD ME ABOUT HERSELF

BY

ANNA CARLOTTA LEFFLER

DUCHESS OF CAJANELLO

A

INTRODUCTION.

IMMEDIATELY after having received the news of Sonia Kovalevsky's sudden and unexpected death, the thought struck me, that it was my duty to continue her Memoirs of her Childhood, published under the title, "Life in Russia (The Sisters Rajevsky)." A duty for several reasons; first, because, anticipating that she would die young, and that I should survive her, she had more than once made me promise to write her biography.

Excessively self-reflecting and self-analysing as she was, she had the habit of brooding over all her feelings, thoughts and actions, and during the three or four years we lived together, in almost daily inter-course, she communicated all these thoughts to me, trying to form her observations into a regular psychological system. This exaggerated tendency to self-contemplation frequently, though unconsciously, led her to disfigure facts. Sharp and merciless as her self-analysis might be, it was sometimes disturbed by a natural inclination to idealising. So the picture she gave differed in several respects from that which others saw.

She judged herself sometimes much more severely, sometimes much more leniently, than others did.

Had she been permitted to carry out her intention of writing the history of her whole life, this image, painted by herself, would have corresponded with the ideas she expressed during her long and frequent psychological conversations with me.

As, unfortunately, this work remained unwritten, which undoubtedly would have been one of the most important biographies in the world's literature, and as it became my lot to draw the feeble outlines of this soul's history, I felt instinctively that the only possible way for me to carry out the task was, so to say, to work under her suggestion, in trying to identify myself with her, as I used to do while she was alive ; to become her second self,—as she often called me,—and to reproduce as far as possible the image she had given me of herself.

However, I allowed more than a year to pass before I could make up my mind to publish these memoirs, which I began to write shortly after her death. During this time I tried to assist my memory by conversation and correspondence with as many of her friends in different countries as I could manage to reach, in order to give a correct statement of the outward events of her life, which she has told me so often. Out of this correspondence I have quoted everything that seemed to throw a true light on her character,—true, in so far as it would agree with her own conception.

So my readers will see it is not a biography true in the objective sense of the word that I am presenting here.

By the by, what is objective truth in speaking of the analysis of the soul?

Many will disagree with my views, and put a very different interpretation on some of Sonia's feelings and actions, but from my standpoint this does not affect me. All the facts I relate are essentially true, so far as I have been capable of verifying them. In this respect I have not followed Sonia's own suggestions, for with regard to facts she was frequently most fantastic.

When, a year ago, I met Henrik Ibsen in Christiania, and told him that I was writing a biography of Sonia Kovalevsky, he said:

'Is it a biography in the true sense of the word, or a poetic image, you are going to give?'

'It is,' I answered, 'her own poem about herself, seen with my eyes, which I mean to write.'

'Quite right,' he said, 'the subject must

be treated poetically.' These words encouraged me, and confirmed my view of the task I had undertaken.

Let others give a realistic description if they can; I only wish to render my individual conception of her own strongly individual analysis of herself.

THE AUTHORESS.

NAPLES, 1892.

I

MAIDEN-DREAMS. MARRIAGE-CEREMONY

WHEN Sonia* was about seventeen, her family spent a winter in St Petersburg.

About this time the intelligent part of the young generation in Russia was stirred by a lively movement, particularly remarkable in the young girls, a movement for promoting mental liberty, development and progress in their native country.

These aspirations were not nihilistic, scarcely even political in their tendency. They arose from a craving for knowledge and light; a craving which had spread so widely, that hundreds of girls of the best families went out to study at foreign universities. As the parents generally opposed this spirit in their daughters, the young women had found a very peculiar and character-

* Diminutive of Sophia.

istic way out of the difficulty, in contracting marriages with young men who shared their views. Once married, they escaped from the parental authority, and were at liberty to go abroad. Many of the female students in Zürich, who were afterwards called home by an imperial ukase on suspicion of nihilism, were married in this way, to men who, after having taken them away from their homes and escorted them to some university, left them there, free and alone, according to mutual agreement.

Now this kind of union was becoming so popular among the friends with whom Sonia and her sister used to associate in St Petersburg, that they came to look upon it as much more ideal than the ordinary marriage-tie between a man and a woman, who in a love-match saw only the satisfaction of individual feelings and sensations, in a word, of self-love.

To these young enthusiasts, personal happiness was a secondary consideration, the sacrifice of self for a common cause being the only great and noble motive. To study, to improve their minds, and devote whatever power they possessed to the benefit of their beloved country, helping it in its hard struggle for freedom, in its progress from darkness and oppression to light and liberty

—this was the idea which inspired the hearts of these young daughters of aristocratic families. Their parents, who had never dreamt of educating them for anything but their destination as ladies and married women, naturally took an uncompromising and hostile position at these signs of independence and rebellion, which now and then burst through the mysterious reticence usually observed by the young in presence of their elders.

'What a happy time!' Sonia used to exclaim when speaking of this period of her life. 'We were so exalted by all these new ideas, so convinced, that the present state of society could not last long, that the glorious time of liberty and general knowledge was quite near, quite certain. And then, what delight in the fellowship of these aspirations! No sooner would two or three young people meet at a party of elders, where they had no right to make themselves heard, than they understood one another immediately by a look, a sigh, an intonation of the voice, and felt that they belonged to one brotherhood.

'What a secret happiness to feel near this young man or woman, whom perhaps you had never seen before, with whom you had scarcely exchanged a few commonplace words, yet who, you knew, was one of the flock, who shared your own ideas and hopes, your own readiness to sacrifice self to the common cause.'

In the society of friends who gathered round Aniuta as their centre, nobody as yet paid any attention to Sonia ; she was six years younger than her sister, and quite a child in appearance. Aniuta allowed her to be present, because she was fond of the little girl, with her green-gooseberry eyes, that would beam with delight at every warm and enthusiastic word spoken by one of her elders, and who, besides, was never intrusive, but kept modestly in the background, behind her older and more brilliant sister.

Sonia thoroughly admired Aniuta, whom she considered in every respect her superior, in beauty, grace, talents and intelligence. But her admiration was mixed with a considerable amount of jealousy, the kind which yearns to equal its object, never to depreciate or lower it. This tendency, which Sonia herself mentions in the recollections of her childhood, was characteristic of her throughout life. She was always inclined to overrate in others the qualities she wished to possess herself, and to repine at the lack of them ; and she was particularly impressed by beauty and pleasant manners. In these advantages her sister seems to have surpassed her considerably, and so Sonia dreamt of eclipsing her on another ground. From her earliest years she had been commended for her cleverness, and her natural love of study and thirst of knowledge were now stimulated by her ambition, and by the encouragement of her teacher in mathematics. She revealed the most remarkably quick understanding, and such a wealth of ideas that her natural gift for scientific work seemed beyond doubt. But her father, whose consent to this kind of study, so unusual for a young girl, had only been given by the persuasion of an old friend of his, who was himself a distinguished scholar, withdrew his approval on the first suspicion that his daughter meant to cultivate these studies in real earnest. Her first timid hints that she would like to go away and study at a foreign university, were as badly received as the discovery some years previously of Aniuta's authorship—in other words, as a criminal tendency to go astray. In fact, the young girls of good families, who had carried out similar plans, were looked upon as nothing less than adventuresses, who brought shame and grief on their parents.

Thus these two antagonistic currents flowed on side by side in this aristocratic home: the hidden, but rebellious and passionate longing for freedom, and the open, honest paternal tyranny, which was convinced of its own legitimacy and superiority, trying to stop and keep under control, to tame and regulate this strange and misunderstood power.

At last Aniuta and one of her friends took a bold resolution. One of them—no matter who —was to contract one of these ideal marriages, which would relieve both ; for if one of them married, they thought the other would be allowed to go abroad with her friend. In this way the journey could scandalise nobody, it would look like a pleasure trip. Sonia would most likely be permitted to join the others, for she was her sister's inseparable shadow, and it was quite out of the question for one sister to travel without the other.

This plan once settled, the next point was to find the right man to help in carrying it out. Aniuta and Inez searched among their acquaintances, and their choice fell upon a young professor at the university, whom they knew but slightly, but of whose honesty and enthusiasm they felt convinced. So one day all three girls—Sonia as usual bringing up the rear— started on their visit to the professor's house.

He was at work in his study when the servant announced the three young ladies, whose visit surprised him, as they did not at all belong to his intimate circle. He rose politely and offered them seats; they sat down, all three on a long sofa, and there was a moment's awkward silence.

The professor was sitting in his rocking-chair, opposite to the young girls, looking at each of them in turn : there was Aniuta, tall, slender, and fair, with her peculiar subtle grace in every movement, her large, radiant, dark blue eyes, which she fixed on him openly, though with a certain hesitation ; then Inez, dark, rather square-built, and somewhat stout, her aquiline nose, hard and clear eyes, looking rather bold; and here was Sonia, with her rich curly hair, her pure regular features, her child-like innocent forehead, and peculiar passionately inquisitive and listening eyes.

At last Aniuta spoke as had been agreed, and without the slightest reluctance put the question : ' Whether the professor might feel inclined to " release " them by entering on a sham marriage with one of them, take them to some university in Germany or Switzerland, and then leave them ? '

In another country, and under other circumstances, a young man would scarcely have re-

ceived such a question from the mouth of a
pretty young girl without putting into his answer
a little gallantry or a tinge of irony. But in this
case the man was equal to the situation—so far
Aniuta had not been mistaken in her choice—
and he answered very seriously and coolly, that
he did not feel in the least disposed to accept
this proposal.

And what about the young girls? You think,
perhaps, they felt humiliated by this refusal? By
no means. Their feminine pride had nothing
whatever to do with this affair, there had been
no idea of pleasing the young man. They received his refusal as calmly as anybody would
have received the answer of some one whom he
had asked to be his travelling companion, and
who had replied 'no' instead of 'yes.'

The three young ladies rose and took leave; the
professor shook hands with them at the door, and
they did not see each other again for many years.
They had not the slightest fear that he would
ever abuse their trust, for they knew that he belonged to the sacred alliance, whose members
could not think of betraying each other. About
fifteen years later, when Sonia Kovalevsky
stood at the height of her fame, she one day, at
a party in St Petersburg, met this man, and

they joked together about the unsuccessful proposal.

One of Aniuta's friends about this time committed the mean action of marrying for love; how they despised and pitied her! Sonia particularly felt her heart swell with indignation that anybody could thus forsake all ideals. And the young wife herself felt thoroughly ashamed in presence of her friends, as if she had fallen deeply. She never dared speak to them about her matrimonial happiness, and she forbade her husband ever to caress her in their presence.

Then, all of a sudden, something quite unexpected happened to Sonia.

Aniuta and Inez, far from being discouraged by their first failure, abode by their plan and chose another young man for their deliverer. He was only an undergraduate, but exceedingly clever, and wished to go to Germany himself in pursuit of his studies. He was of good family, and generally considered very promising; so it seemed probable that the respective parents, whether Aniuta's or Inez's, would have no serious objection to the union. This time the proposal was made in a less solemn way; Aniuta, profiting by an opportunity, when she met him in the house of mutual friends, put the question to him in the course of their conversation. He answered, quite unexpectedly, that he felt very much inclined to enter upon the scheme, only with this change in the programme, that he wished Sonia for his wife.

This, however, caused much anxiety to the three allies; how could they possibly persuade the father to give away this child, especially as her six-year-older sister was still unmarried? If an acceptable 'parti' for the eldest daughter had been proposed, they knew quite well that her father would not have been adverse to it. Indeed, Aniuta gave him much anxiety through her fanciful, unaccountable character, and she was of an age when a young girl ought to marry. No doubt Kovalevsky was rather young, but his prospects seemed very hopeful, and he would not have been at all unwelcome as a suitor to the elder daughter. But Sonia! No. The offer was refused absolutely and without appeal, and the family prepared at once to return to Palibino.

What was to be done? To go back into the country, to give up all hope, to say good-bye to all interests which had become the essence of life to the young girls—was like going into prison without feeling that they were martyrs

for a great cause. It would have been easier to
suffer real imprisonment for their ideals than
such unpoetic exile.

In this dilemma, Sonia, usually so shy, took a
great and decisive step. The tender little girl,
who could scarcely bear an unkind look, a dis-
approving word from those she loved, became
like steel at this critical moment. Naturally
very sensitive and affectionate, fond of caresses
like a dog that clings fondly to any one who in-
vites it by a kind glance, when once her spirit of
resistance was roused, she could show an un-
bending energy and hardness; regardless of all
feeling, she could deeply wound the very person
whom, a moment before, she had overwhelmed
with marks of the tenderest affection. There
was in her an intensity of will-power, a consuming energy, even where her feelings were not
concerned at all. Now her mind was made up
to get out, away from home, to continue her
studies—cost what it might.

There was to be a family dinner-party. In
the morning her mother was out shopping, her
father at his club, and her governess helping the
maid to decorate the drawing-room. The girls
were alone in their room, their fine new dresses
lying ready to put on for dinner.

They were never allowed to go out of the house unattended ; but to-day Sonia, profiting by the general stir and bustle, stole out alone. Aniuta, who was in the plot, went down stairs with her, and kept watch at the gate till her sister was out of sight, after which she returned to her own room in anxious expectation, and began putting on her light blue dress.

It was dusk already, and the first gas-lamps were lighted.

Sonia had pulled down her veil, and tied her bashlik close round her cheeks ; she walked with long strides down the broad streets, which at this hour were almost empty—the first time she found herself there alone. Her pulses were hammering with the extreme excitement which makes grand enterprises so attractive to young, romantically-inclined hearts. She felt herself the heroine of a romance which was going to be acted ; she, little Sonia, who had hitherto been the shadow of her sister. Still, this romance was very different from the usual love stories, which she despised.

It was not to a lovers' tryst she went with her firm, quick, rhythmical step ; it was not the excitement of love which made her heart beat so quickly, as, holding her breath, madly afraid of the darkness, like a child, she hurried up the unlighted stairs to the third floor of a gloomy house in a by-street. She gave three little quick nervous knocks at a door, which was so instantly opened, that evidently the young man who now received her must have been watching for her arrival. He immediately led her into a modest study, where books were piled upon tables and chairs, and where a shaky sofa had been cleared for the occasion, that she might find a place to sit down.

It must be confessed that the young man did not look like a hero of romance. His bristling red beard, and too big nose, made him appear ugly at first sight ; but when you caught a glance from his deep dark blue eyes, you met an expression so intelligent, kind, and benevolent, that you could not help feeling attracted. Towards the young girl who had trusted him in such a peculiar way, his manners were entirely those of an elder brother.

The young couple were now waiting in great excitement, listening intently for quick angry steps in the passage, and more than once Sonia started from the sofa, crimson and white with emotion, when she thought somebody was coming.

In the mean time her parents had come home,
but they had only just time to dress before the
guests arrived, so they did not notice their
youngest daughter's absence till all were
gathered in the dining-room, ready to sit down
to table.

'Where is Sonia?' they both at once asked
Aniuta, who looked quite pale; at this moment
she appeared even taller and more self-conscious
than usual, with an expression of defiance, mixed
with excitement and expectation.

'Sonia has gone out,' she answered in a low
voice, trying in vain to prevent its vibration, and
evading her father's eye.

'Gone out! What do you mean? With
whom?'

'By herself. There is a note on her toilet-
table.'

A servant was sent at once to fetch the note;
the party sat down to dinner in deep silence.

Sonia had dealt her blow better than she probably knew herself, more cruelly than she could
have dreamed of. In her childish spite, with the
heedless selfishness of youth, which has no mercy,
because it does not realise the pain it gives, she
had hurt her father in his tenderest point.

In presence of all his relations this proud man

had to swallow his humiliation at his daughter's scandal. She had only written these words :—

'Father, forgive me, I am with Woldemar, and I ask you not to oppose our marriage any longer.'

Ivan Sergejevitsch read these lines in silence, then, muttering an excuse, he rose from table.

Ten minutes later, Sonia and her companion, who were listening with increasing anxiety, heard the angry steps they expected ; the unlocked door was flung open without a knock, and General Krukovsky stood before his trembling daughter.

Towards the close of the dinner father and daughter entered the dining-room together, followed by Woldemar Kovalevsky. Ivan Sergejevitsch said with trembling voice :

'Allow me to introduce to you the future husband of my daughter Sonia.'

II

AT THE UNIVERSITY

THIS was the dramatic introduction to Sonia's strange wedded life, according to her own statement. Her parents forgave her, and shortly after—in October 1868—the marriage was celebrated at Palibino.

The young couple started for St Petersburg, and here Kovalevsky immediately introduced his wife to the political circles which had been the object of her ardent longings. A friend who became very intimate with her afterwards, gives the following description of her appearance at this time:

'Amongst all these political ladies who were more or less worn with life's cares and struggles, she seemed quite a phenomenon; and because of her childlike appearance she got the pet name of "The little sparrow."'

She was only just eighteen, but looked much

younger. She was of small and slender stature, though her face was rather full; she had short, curly chestnut hair, lively features, sparkling eyes which continually changed their expression, altogether a striking mixture of childlike naïveté and depth of thought. She attracted everybody by the unconscious grace which distinguished her at this period of her life; old and young, men and women, all were charmed. Most natural in her manners, without a shadow of coquetry, she did not seem to have any idea of the general homage of which she was the object. In fact, she paid no attention at all to her appearance, or to her dress, which was as plain as possible, even a little untidy—a shortcoming which she never corrected. Her friend says: 'I remember one day, during a most animated conversation, she kept fumbling with the trimming of her left sleeve, of which some stitches were undone, and after having pulled it off altogether, she threw it on the floor, as if pleased to get rid of it.'

The young couple spent six months in St Petersburg, and then went to Heidelberg, where Sonia wished to study mathematics, and her husband geology. They entered their names as students at the university, and afterwards went to England for their summer vacation. There Sonia had the opportunity of making the acquaintance of many celebrities: George Eliot, Darwin, Spencer, Huxley, etc.

In George Eliot's diary, published in her biography by Mr J. W. Cross, there is a note dated October 5th, 1869:

'On Sunday, an interesting Russian pair came to see us—M. and Madame Kovilevsky (*sic*): she, a pretty creature, with charming modest voice and speech, who is studying mathematics (by allowance through the aid of Kirchhoff) at Heidelberg; he, amiable and intelligent, studying the concrete sciences apparently—especially geology: and about to go to Vienna for six months for this purpose, leaving his wife at Heidelberg!' (*George Eliot's Life*, vol. iii. p. 101.)

This plan, however, was not immediately carried out, and Woldemar spent a term in Heidelberg with his wife. Their life at that time is described in the following way by the friend I have mentioned, who, through Sonia's intervention, had obtained permission from her parents to study with her:

'Some days after my arrival in Heidelberg, in October 1869, Sonia returned from England with her husband. She seemed quite happy, and very pleased with her journey. Fresh and healthy, with rosy cheeks, she was as charming as when I saw her first; but there was even more life and fire in her eyes, she felt renewed energy to take up and continue her recently commenced studies.

' However, this serious occupation did not prevent her from enjoying everything else, even the merest trifles. I remember distinctly the walk she and I took alone together the day after their arrival, racing along the road just like children. How charming and refreshing are these memories of the beginning of our university life! Sonia seemed so happy, so nobly happy; and yet in after-times, when she spoke of her youth, it was with a bitter regret, as if she had wasted her young years altogether. This always made me think of those first months in Heidelberg, of our enthusiastic discussions, of her poetical relation to her young husband, who in those days loved her with an entirely platonic tenderness. She seemed to love him in the same way; both were as yet ignorant of those lower passions which are usually misnamed love. It seems to me that Sonia had no reason to complain; her mind was full of high aspirations. Yet this was the only period during which I ever knew her happy. A little later, in the very next year, it was no longer the s me.

The lectures began immediately after our arrival. During the day we were all three at the university, and in the evening we studied at home. We had scarcely ever time to walk, except on Sundays. Sometimes we went to Mannheim to see a play at the theatre. We had very few acquaintances, and on the whole paid very few visits.

'Sonia immediately attracted her teachers' attention by her unusual capacity for mathematics. Professor Königsberger, the celebrated natural philosopher Kirchhof, whose courses of practical physical science she attended, in fact everybody, spoke of her as something extraordinary. She had become so famous in the little town, that people would stop in the streets to look after the remarkable Russian lady. One day she came home laughing, and told me that a woman with a child on her arm had stopped and looked at her, saying quite loud to the child : " Look, look, that is the girl who is so fond of going to school." (Sieh, sieh, das ist das Mädchen was so fleissig in die Schule geht !)

'Reticent, almost shy, as she was in her intercourse with teachers and students, Sonia always

entered the university with downcast or far-away-
looking eyes. She never spoke to her fellow-
students when she could help it. These manners
highly pleased the German professors. And her
shyness was by no means simulated, it was perfectly natural to her at that age. I remember
her coming home one day and telling me that
she had discovered a mistake which had been
made by one of the professors or pupils in a
demonstration on the black board. He got
more and more confused, and could not possibly
find the fault. With violently beating heart
Sonia at last made up her mind to get up and
point out the mistake.

'Kovalevsky used to take a lively interest in
everything, which made him a very pleasant ·
companion. However, our happy life was not to
last long. At the beginning of winter Sonia's
sister and her friend Inez arrived. Both were
several years older than we. As our apartments were rather small, Kovalevsky thought he
had better find lodgings elsewhere, and leave his
room to the new comers. Sonia often visited
him, and sometimes spent whole days in his
company; they also took walks alone together.
Very naturally, it was not pleasant for them to
be continually surrounded by so many ladies,

especially as the two elder ones were not always
very amiable to Kovalevsky. They had their
own ideas, and thought that, as the marriage had
only been an outward ceremony, Kovalevsky had
no right to give a more intimate character to his
relations with Sonia. This interference on their
part caused friction now and then, and marred
the harmony which had hitherto prevailed in our
little circle.

'After having spent a term in this way,
Kovalevsky preferred to leave Heidelberg, where
he had ceased to feel happy. He first went
to Jena, then to Munich, and gave himself up
entirely to his studies. He was very clever,
most industrious, and frugal in his habits, without the slightest desire for amusements. Sonia
used to say that all he wanted to make him
happy was a book and a glass of tea. She did
not quite like this, and began to get jealous of
his studies, thinking that his work seemed to
make up entirely for her society. Sometimes
we would go and see her husband with her,
and between the terms the two took journeys
together, which always gave her great pleasure.
However, Sonia could not reconcile herself to
being separated from him during the terms,
and she began to torment him with incessant

demands. She could not travel alone, he was to come and fetch her, and take her wherever she wanted to go; while he was most absorbed in his work, she gave him commissions, and expected him to help her with all those trifles he had been in the habit of attending to most amiably, but which now seemed to irritate him.

'When in aftertimes Sonia spoke to me about her past life, her bitterest complaint was: "Nobody has really loved me!" And when I objected, But your husband did love you most fondly and truly, she always said, "He only loved me when I was with him, but he could do quite well without me."

'To me it seemed very natural, that he should prefer not to be continually in her presence, under the existing circumstances; but Sonia could not see this. From her childhood she had been rather fond of carrying everything to extremes. She wished to possess without being possessed. I think this was to a great extent the origin of her life's tragedy.'

I shall add a few more observations by her friend and fellow-student during those years, which will show that these peculiarities of her character were developed from her earliest youth, and were the root of all her subsequent conflicts and sufferings :

'She was immensely fond of success; when once she had a settled purpose before her, nothing could stop her in pursuing it with any means at her disposal, and so she always used to reach her end. Only where feelings were concerned, strangely enough, her keen perception continually failed her. She claimed too much from those who loved her, and whom she loved, and she had a way of taking by force what would have been readily given, if she had not so imperiously claimed it. She had an intense craving for tenderness and confidence, and continually wanted somebody at her side to share everything with her, but she rendered life impossible to those who lived in close contact with her. Hers was a nature much too restless and inharmonious to be contented in the long run with intimate and tender companionship. Moreover, she was much too personal to have sufficient regard for the individuality of her companion.

'Kovalevsky, too, in his way, was of a very unsettled nature, always full of new schemes and ideas. God knows whether these two remarkably gifted persons would have been able under any circumstances whatever to lead a happy life together for any length of time.

'Sonia spent two terms at Heidelberg, till the autumn of 1870, when she went to Berlin to continue her studies under the direction of Professor Weierstrass.

'In the mean time her husband had obtained his degree as Dr. phil. in Jena, by means of a dissertation which created a great sensation, and acquired him a name as a distinguished and independent investigator.'

III

STUDIES WITH WEIERSTRASS. VISIT TO PARIS DURING THE COMMUNE

ONE day Professor Weierstrass was rather surprised to see a young lady present herself before him, asking to be admitted as his pupil in mathematics. The Berlin University was, and still is, closed to women, but Sonia's ardent desire to be taught by the man who was generally acknowledged to be the father of modern mathematical analysis, made her apply to him for private lessons.

Professor Weierstrass felt a certain distrust in seeing this unknown female applicant; however, he promised to try her, and gave her some of the problems which he had set apart for the more advanced pupils in the seminary for mathematics. He felt convinced that she would not be able to solve them, and forgot all about her, the more so as her outward appearance on the first visit had left no impression at all upon his mind. She never dressed well, and on this occasion she wore a hat which hid her face completely, and made her look very old, so that Professor Weierstrass, as he told me himself, after having seen her for the first time, had neither the slightest idea of her age, nor of her unusually expressive eyes, which used to attract everybody at first sight. A week later she called again, and said that she had solved all the problems. He did not believe her, but asked her to sit down beside him, after which he began to examine her solutions one by one. To his great surprise everything was not only correct, but very acute and ingenious. Now in her eagerness she took off her hat and uncovered her short curly hair; she blushed at his praises, and the elderly professor felt something like fatherly tenderness towards this young woman, who possessed the divination of genius to a degree he had seldom found, even in his more advanced male pupils. And from that moment the great mathematician became her friend for life, the most faithful and helpful friend she could wish. In his family she was received as a daughter and sister.

The four years' work that now ensued with Professor Weierstrass had a decisive influence on her whole scientific career. Her productions are based upon his, they are applications or developments of his maxims.

The lessons were carried on in this way: he visited her once a week, and every Sunday evening she came to him. Her husband, who had accompanied her to Berlin, left her alone there with her fellow-student from Heidelberg, but now and then he came and visited her. Their relations were still very peculiar, and caused some wonder in the Weierstrass family, where the husband never appeared, in spite of the familiar footing on which his wife stood with all its members. Sonia never mentioned him, never introduced him to Weierstrass, but on Sunday evenings, after her lesson, he would ring the door bell and say to the servant: 'Will you tell Madame Kovalevsky that a carriage is waiting for her at the door.' Sonia always felt rather awkward at the unnatural relations in which they stood to one another. One of the Heidelberg professors said that he once met Kovalevsky at her house, and that she introduced him as a 'relative.'

Her friend gives the following description of

their life in Berlin :—'We led a much more solitary and monotonous life than in Heidelberg, and were quite alone. Sonia used to sit bent over her papers all day long, I was at the laboratory till the evening, and after a hurried supper we resumed our work. Except Professor Weierstrass, who came frequently, we never saw anybody within our walls. Sonia was depressed, nothing seemed to give her pleasure, she was indifferent to everything except her work. Her husband's visits used to cheer her a little, though as a rule their pleasure in being together was spoilt by misunderstandings and reproaches. Nevertheless they seemed much attached to one another. They always took long walks by themselves.

'When alone with me, Sonia never went out, neither for walks nor to the play, not even for the most indispensable shopping.

'We were invited to spend Christmas with the Weierstrass family, and a tree had been decked for our sake only. Sonia was in urgent need of a new dress, but could not be induced to go and buy one. We had a severe quarrel on this occasion. (If her husband had been present, it would have been all right; he used to provide for all her wants, to choose the material, and decide the fashion of her dresses.) At last she gave our landlady a commission to buy the stuff and order the dress to be made, without herself setting foot outside the door.

'It was most extraordinary how she could go on hour after hour with the most fatiguing brainwork, without once rising from her writing-table. When, after a whole day's work, she would at last leave her papers and get up, she was frequently so absorbed in her thoughts, that she kept striding up and down her room, speaking out loud to herself, and sometimes bursting into a laugh. At those moments her imagination had carried her far away from the real world; but she could never be persuaded to tell what fancies had filled her mind. She slept very little at night and very restlessly. Sometimes she would start up violently, awaking from some fantastic dream, and ask me to keep her company. She used to tell me her dreams, which were always peculiar and interesting. Frequently they were a kind of visions, which she took for prophecies, and events often justified her belief. Her temperament was nervous in the highest degree. She was never at rest, would always be occupied with some difficult task or problem, exerting herself to the utmost to master it, and yet I never saw her so prostrate as when she had gained her end. Reality always seemed far behind her anticipations. While she was thus overstraining her nerves, her companionship was not particularly pleasant, but when the strain was over, and you saw her depressed and miserable in the midst of her triumphs, you could not help pitying her intensely. It was these strong contrasts between light and shadow which made her character so interesting.

'On the whole, our life in Berlin—with bad lodgings, bad food, ditto air, constant and excessive work, no changes, no amusements—was so dreary, that I frequently looked back to our first time in Heidelberg as to a lost paradise. When, in the autumn of 1874, Sonia got her degree as Dr. phil. she was so worn out mentally and physically, that on her return to Russia, she was for a long time incapable of any work.

'In fact, Sonia's scientific labours never gave her any real joy. She would always go to the utmost limit of exertion, which prevented her, not only from enjoying life, but from enjoying her very work; thought was her tyrant instead of her servant. It was quite the reverse later on with her literary productions, which used to give her intense delight and put her into the most cheerful humour.

'Many other circumstances besides her excessive work added to the unhappiness of her student years in Berlin.

'First of all, her relation to her husband, her sense of the false position in which they were placed, and which had become worse through the unwise interference of her parents.

'They had visited her several times during her vacations, and taken her with them to Russia. When at last the real state of things had become clear to them, they had blamed her and tried to improve matters by bringing husband and wife into closer relations; but Sonia would not hear of any change.

'Yet she was not satisfied with her isolated life. Already she had begun to feel the craving for great emotions, which afterwards became a consuming fire in her. Her innermost self was the very reverse of what you would suppose, judging by her way of living; but her longings and desires were suppressed, partly from shyness, partly from lack of practical sense and a feeling of her false position. Later on she often bitterly regretted the utter solitude in which she had spent these years.

'The two friends' helplessness in all practical matters went a long way to render their life unpleasant; they always got bad lodgings, miserable food, and the worst servants. Once they fell into the clutches of a gang of thieves, who robbed them systematically. On another occasion, discovering that their servant was a thief, they taxed her with it; she grew insolent, and they had to give her notice immediately. When they were sitting alone in their room that evening, not knowing how to get their beds made for the night, somebody knocked at the window (they lived on the ground floor). They looked up and saw a woman's face against the pane. In great fright they asked what she wanted, and she replied that she was looking for a situation. Although they disliked her appearance very much, they were too helpless to refuse, and with great misgivings engaged her. This woman tyrannised over and robbed them to such a degree, that they had to call in the police to get rid of her.

'However, as a rule, Sonia was very indifferent to the practical sides of life; she scarcely noticed whether her food was good or bad, her rooms done or not, or her clothes torn or tidy. It was only during serious crises that such unpleasant things affected her.'

In January 1871, Sonia was obliged to interrupt her studies to start on a very adventurous journey.

*　　　*　　　*　　　*　　　*

Aniuta, who soon wearied of her monotonous life in Heidelberg, had gone to Paris without her parents' permission. She wanted to train herself for the career of an authoress, and felt that living shut up in a study with Sonia did not suit her purpose. What she required was acquaintances among literary people, knowledge of real life and of the stage. Once escaped from the paternal restraint, she boldly followed her own devices. As she could not possibly write to her father that she was in Paris, her passionate craving for living life on her own responsibility induced her to deceive him. So her letters always went through Sonia's hands, and bore the German stamp. But gradually she was drawn into relations, which entangled her so completely, that she could not release herself, and every day it became more difficult to confess the truth to her parents.

She had formed an intimate connection with a young Frenchman, who afterwards took a leading position under the Commune; and she now found herself shut up in Paris during the whole siege.

Sonia, in the greatest anxiety about her sister's fate, and oppressed by her responsibility in having helped Aniuta in her secret journey, made up her mind, as soon as the siege had been raised, to try to get into Paris accompanied by her husband, and to search for her sister.

When in after times Sonia spoke of this journey, she was hardly able to explain how they succeeded in getting into the city, breaking through the German lines. They walked along the Seine till they discovered an empty boat which had been pulled ashore. They immediately took possession of it and set off, but had scarcely gone a few yards when a sentry caught sight of them and gave the alarm. Without answering they hurried on, and owing either to negligence or indifference on the part of the guards, they succeeded in escaping to the opposite shore, and in entering Paris unnoticed, just at the first outbreak of the Commune.

Years afterwards, Sonia had an idea of publishing some of their experiences in literary form ; but, alas, this plan, as well as many others, went to the grave with her. One of her ideas was to write a story with the title: 'The Sisters Rajevsky during the Commune,' and amongst other interesting scenes, to describe a night in an ambulance where she and Aniuta did service, and where they met some young girls of their early acquaintance in St Petersburg. While shells were exploding all around, and wounded persons were constantly being brought in, the young women talked in a whisper about past times, which were so different from their present life and surroundings; it all seemed like a dream or a fairy tale.

Sonia was still at the age when grand and thrilling historical events impress one like a sensation novel; she saw bombs bursting without the slightest fear, it only gave her a pleasant feeling of excitement, an inward exultation, to live in the midst of this drama.

This time she could do nothing for her sister. Aniuta had flung herself with passionate energy into the political movement, and wished for no better fate than to risk her life with the man to whom she had united her lot for ever. So, shortly after these events, the Kovalevskys left Paris again, and Sonia resumed her studies in Berlin.

But after the fall of the Commune she was

called back, this time by Aniuta herself, who
now besought her to intercede with their father
in order to induce him to forgive her deception,
and to use all possible influence to help her out
of the desperate situation in which she was
placed. Mr. Y. had been taken prisoner, and
was condemned to death.

When we remember the portrait Sonia has
given of her father in 'The Sisters Rajevsky,'
we can easily imagine how painfully he felt
the blow when he suddenly learned the cruel
truth, that he had again been deceived by his
children, that his elder daughter had followed
her inclination, and gone her own way in
a manner which must necessarily wound all
his instincts and principles in their tenderest
point. Only a few years previously, on discovering Aniuta's secret authorship, for which
she received payment, he had been beside
himself with grief and anger, and had broken
out into these words: 'Now you sell your
work, how can I be certain that some day you
will not sell yourself!'

Strangely enough, he took this new and far
deeper grief much more calmly. He and his
wife hastened to Paris, accompanied by the
Kovalevskys, and on meeting his guilty child

he was so full of kindness and forbearance, that his daughters, who felt what they had deserved of him, from this moment clung to him with an affection they had never shown before.

To my regret, I can only give a few unconnected anecdotes relating to this most eventful period.

As General Krukovsky had an introduction to Thiers, he applied to him to obtain pardon for his future son-in-law. Thiers was sorry not to be able to do anything, but in the course of their conversation he let fall the apparently trivial remark, that the prisoners, among whom was M. T., would be removed to another prison on the following day; they were to pass by a building where an exhibition was held, and where there was apt to be great traffic at that time of the day. Consequently Aniuta went thither at the appointed hour, mixed with the crowd, and at the moment when the prisoners passed, stole unnoticed through the escort of soldiers, seized Mr Y.'s arm, and disappeared with him into the exhibition, whence they succeeded in escaping through another gate to the railway station.

The story seems strange, almost incredible, but I simply state it as it was told by Sonia and other friends.

After a friend's death, how bitterly do we often regret not having paid sufficient attention to his or her words, not having put down all the interesting things they said. There is the more reason for me to deplore my negligence in this case, as Sonia so often said to me: 'You are to write my biography after my death.' But in those moments of intimate conversation, who realises that the day may actually come, when we are left behind, and have nothing but the memory of the close tie that bound us to the deceased? Who does not expect a morrow to come which will offer abundant opportunity for filling up the blanks left in our conversation, with its rapid transitions from one subject to another?

In 1874, Sonia took her degree as Dr. phil. at the University of Göttingen, for which she had written three dissertations under the direction of Weierstrass, of which one in particular—'Zur Theorie der partiellen Differentialgleichungen' (*Crelle's Journal*, vol. 80), is considered one of her most remarkable works. By special licence, the oral examination was pretermitted. In the following letter to the Dean of the Faculty of Philosophy at Göttingen, she explains in her own characteristic way her motives for desiring the dispensation, which is only granted in very exceptional cases :—

'Your Honour (Euer Spectabilität) will kindly permit me to add a few words to the petition by which I present myself for the degree of Dr. phil. in your faculty.

'It is not an easy step for me to come forward from the retirement in which I have been living hitherto. I have overcome my reluctance to do so only from a desire to satisfy very near relatives of mine, whose judgment is of great importance to me, and to whom I wanted to give an indisputable proof that my taste for the study of mathematics was really serious, and that my work has not been in vain. Moreover, I have been told that as a foreigner I may take my degree *in absentia*, provided I present sufficiently important works, and favourable testimonials from competent authorities.

'And also—I hope your Honour will not misunderstand my open confession—I am doubtful whether I possess sufficient self-assertion for an *examen rigorosum*; I am rather afraid that my exceptional position before a tribunal of unknown gentlemen would be somewhat oppressive and confusing to me, though I am perfectly convinced that my examiners would meet me with kind consideration.

'As a last reason I must add, that I have not mastered the German language sufficiently in conversation, though I am accustomed to use it in mathematics, when I have ample time for reflection.

'I did not begin to learn German till five years ago, and during the four years I have spent in Berlin, I have lived a very solitary life, scarcely speaking the language except during the hours I was with my dear master.

'For these reasons, I venture to ask for your Honour's kind permission that I may be dispensed from *examen rigorosum.*'

This request, and particularly the great merits of her written work, as well as her excellent testimonials, succeeded in obtaining for Sonia the exceptional favour of being created Dr. phil. without personal attendance.

Shortly after the Krukovsky family were again united in their old family home, Palibino.

IV

LIFE IN RUSSIA

VERY different indeed is the present picture of the family from the description Sonia has given in the memoirs of her childhood ('Sisters Rajevsky'). The two young girls, dreaming of the wide unknown world, had now changed into highly-experienced women. Though their youthful anticipations had scarcely been realised, they had seen and heard enough to have plenty of subjects for conversation during the winter evenings at their fireside in the large drawing-room with the red silk damask furniture, whilst the samovar was singing on the tea-table, and the starving wolves were performing their nightly concert outside in the lonely park. The world had lost something of its immensity in their eyes, for they had seen a good deal of it, and measured its proportions.

Aniuta had passed through a sufficiently

eventful time to satisfy her longing for strong emotions. She was passionately fond of the man who sat at her side in the arm-chair, with a tired, somewhat satirical expression ; her love was so intense and jealous, that it promised to offer constant and sufficient excitement. The younger sister, hitherto, it is true, had only lived in her intelligence, but her thirst for knowledge had been so completely satisfied, nay, satiated, that she was incapable at present of working any more with her brain. She spent her time in reading novels, playing cards, and mixing in the society of the neighbourhood, where intellectual interests were scarcely cultivated at all.

The greatest source of joy to Sonia at this time was the change that had taken place in her father. Like herself, he was one of those who, through intelligence and reflection, are able to modify and improve their character, and the roughness and despotism, which used formerly to be characteristic of him, had been softened under the hard trials to which his daughters had subjected him. He discovered by experience, that such power as he had claimed to exercise in his younger years cannot be arrogated with impunity, even by parents over their children. So he now tolerated with indulgence the radical opinions of one son-in-law, a former 'Communard,' as well as the materialistic tendencies of his other son-in-law, the naturalist.

This was the most beautiful memory Sonia kept of her father, and it impressed itself the more deeply in her heart, as this winter was his last ; heart-disease put a quick and unexpected end to his life.

The blow was very hard. Of late Sonia had attached herself so fondly to her father, whom, indeed, she had always loved more than her mother. Madame Krukovsky was one of those women whom everybody likes, and who are kind to all, but who, for this very reason, was less congenial to her daughter. Moreover, Sonia always imagined herself to be loved by her mother less than her brother and sister, while she knew she was her father's favourite.

His death left a terrible blank, and made her feel very lonely. Aniuta had her husband, with whom she could share her grief; Sonia had nobody. She had always kept aloof from the man whose most ardent desire had been to comfort and help her. Now, suddenly, her relation to him appeared more painful and unnatural to her than ever, her longing for tenderness broke down all prejudices, and so, in this time of sorrow, she prepared herself quietly to become his real wife.

. . . . .

Next winter the whole family moved to St Petersburg. Sonia soon found herself the centre of a most distinguished and intellectual circle, an exquisite society, the equal of which is hardly to be found anywhere but in the capital of Russia. Not only Sonia, but any one who has frequented similar circles, will acknowledge that really distinguished and liberal-minded Russians surpass all others in manysidedness, unbiassed views, and a wide spiritual sphere. They are ahead of the most advanced in other countries, the first to discover new mental phenomena on the horizon, and with their wonderfully open eye they combine an enthusiasm for, and a faith in, their ideals, which we scarcely find in any other European nation.

Here Sonia felt herself understood and admired. For her, now in the full bloom of youth, this change was delightful; she threw herself ardently into the vortex of the world—festivals, plays, lectures, parties, and similar excitements.

As her present surroundings were more given to literary than to scientific interests, Sonia, with her responsive sympathy, was carried away into the same groove. She contributed to newspapers, wrote poetry, dramatic criticism, etc., always anonymously; she also published a novel, 'The Private Lecturer,' which treated of university life in a small German town, and was considered very promising.

Aniuta, who also settled down in Petersburg with her husband for some years, became a really successful authoress. Woldemar Kovalevsky worked chiefly at translations, and published several popular scientific works, Brehm's celebrated 'Birds,' for example.

The fortune Sonia inherited from her father was very small at present, as he had left the bulk of his property to his wife; and the life the Kovalevskys were leading necessitated a certain luxury. This may have given Sonia the first idea of throwing herself into business speculations. Though her husband was personally indifferent to all kinds of luxury, his lively and impressionable imagination was soon carried away by these ideas, and so one industrial enterprise followed another. They built houses in St Petersburg, bathing establishments, an orangery; they edited papers, started inventions of different kinds, and for a time everything seemed to flourish. Their friends prophesied a glorious future, and when in 1878 their first and only child was born, this daughter was hailed as a great heiress. But, as usual, Sonia had ominous forebodings of misfortunes. One of her intimate friends at the time remembers, that on the very day when there was to be a grand ceremony in honour of their first house, of which the foundation stone was to be laid, Sonia said, that the day was spoilt for her by a dream she had had the previous night. She had seen herself standing on the site of the new house, surrounded by a large crowd which had assembled to witness the ceremony; all of a sudden people had separated, and in the midst of them her husband had appeared, fighting with a diabolical man, who fell upon him, and with a sardonic laugh, knocked him down.

For a long time she remained uneasy and downhearted on account of this dream, which was to be most sadly fulfilled.

When all their speculations, after having been started in the grandest style, failed one after another, Sonia's energy and strength of mind revealed themselves in all their superiority. For a moment she might be tempted to use her intelligence and inventive power for the purpose of creating a fortune, but her heart could never deeply attach itself to such an unsatisfactory pursuit. To lose millions at one stroke would not disturb her night's rest, or add a wrinkle to her brow, and she now beheld the loss of a dream-fortune without the slightest grief. She had wished to be rich, because all manifestations of life tempted her, because her imaginative and passionate nature made her wish to know everything. But when she saw that all attempts failed, she was instantly ready to give them up; and now she devoted all her energy to comfort and help her husband.

Strangely enough, this unassuming man, who had never for a moment wished for riches, or been tempted by the treasures they can procure, had been much more ardent than his wife in his desire to make a fortune in this way. It seemed as if failure in itself would crush his nature, while Sonia possessed, not only the rare strength of submitting to the inevitable, but also sufficient elasticity of mind to throw herself into new tasks.

This time she succeeded in preventing a collapse. Regardless of effort and humiliation, she hurried to all their friends who had shared in the enterprises, and an arrangement was made which satisfied all parties. She was rewarded by her husband's gratitude and admiration, and a new era of happiness seemed to dawn upon them.

But the demon of Sonia's dream now really made his appearance. He was a kind of adventurer in grand style, with whom Kovalevsky had had business relations, and who now tried to tempt him into new and dangerous speculations. Sonia, who possessed to an unusual degree the gift of penetrating character at first sight, immediately took such a dislike to this man, that she could not bear to see him in her house. She besought her husband to keep aloof from this bad adviser, to give up all speculations, as she had done herself, and to return to scientific work. But it was no use. Although about this time, 1880–81, Kovalevsky was appointed Professor of Palæontology at the University of Moscow, where he and his wife were then residing, he could not tear himself away from his grand schemes, which were taking more and more fantastic dimensions.

Kovalevsky was so blinded by his new and dangerous ally, that he would not listen to his wife's objections. At last, as he could not make her share his views, he excluded her from his confidence, and acted on his own responsibility

This was the most painful blow to her, and one which, with her character, she was unable to bear. Having once made up her mind really to belong to her husband, she had staked everything on tightening and deepening the bond between them. It was in her nature to devote herself with passionate intensity to that which, at any given moment, she felt to be the most important object of her life. She drew a distinct line between the important and the unimportant, and it was one of the great features in her character, which rendered her so superior to other women, that she never sacrificed the essential to the unessential. There was no narrowness in her; in matters of feeling she could not bear half-heartedness, and she was capable of sacrificing all to the one great purpose in view.

Sonia did her utmost to save her husband from the danger that threatened him. One of her friends describes her struggles and sacrifices in the following way :—

' She tried to give Kovalevsky a new interest in his science, occupied herself with geological studies, prepared his lectures with him, did everything to render his home-life as attractive as possible. All in vain. I think he was no longer in a normal state of mind; his nerves had been over-excited, and he could not recover the lost balance.'

The adventurer had no more ardent wish than to separate the too clear-sighted wife from her husband, and he profited by the dawning discontent between them, to make her suspect that her husband's reticence had another cause than she supposed, and that she had reason to be jealous.

From Sonia's own statements we know, that as a child of ten she had a tendency to passionate jealousy. To touch this chord was to rouse the strongest passion of her ardent nature. Sonia lost her critical insight, and was incapable of examining whether the accusation was true or not—in later years she was almost positive that the whole thing was an invention—she only felt an intense desire to get away, away from the humiliation of feeling herself abandoned, a fear lest her passion should tempt her to base espionage, or to making a scandal. To live with a husband whose love and confidence she thought she had lost, to see him go to ruin without being able to stop him, was a task beyond her nature. She was incapable of resigning; in matters of feeling she was as uncompromising and exacting as she was forbearing and easy to satisfy in outward matters. Without really loving this man, she had devoted herself entirely to him, shared all his interests, and tried to attach him to her with the ardent desire of a woman, who naturally craves for possessing the undivided devotion of her husband and her child's father. When, in spite of all these efforts, she saw him turn away and place another between them, the artificial bond of tenderness burst asunder, her heart shrank back and cast out the image to which it had clung by an effort of her will, and she was once more alone.

She now resolved to create a future for herself and her little daughter, and left home and country to resume her solitary, studious life abroad.

V.

A TRAVELLING ADVENTURE. A
BLOW OF FATE.

WHEN the train had left the station, and Sonia
had lost the last glimpse of the friends who
had seen her off, she yielded to her emotion,
which hitherto she had repressed by a strong
effort, and burst into a violent fit of tears. She
wept for her short happiness, for her lost dream
of fully sympathetic life with another person ;
and she trembled at the prospect of lonely study,
which had once been her whole life, but which
could satisfy her no longer, now that she had
tasted the happiness of living in a home of her
own, loved and understood by sympathising
friends.

She tried to find comfort in the thought that
she was going to resume her mathematical
studies, that she would write a work which was
to bring her fame and to shed glory over her

sex—it was all in vain ; these joys now seemed pale compared to the personal happiness, which for the last few years had been her lot and only aim. The paroxysm of grief became more and more violent, and shook her from head to foot.

She never noticed a middle-aged gentleman, who was sitting opposite to her, watching her with sympathy. 'I cannot bear to see you cry in this way,' he exclaimed at last. 'I suppose it is the first time you have been out into the world alone, but after all, you are not going to cannibals, and a young girl like you may always be sure to find friends when she wants them.'

Sonia looked up in surprise, and immediately stopped crying. She who used to conceal so carefully the wounds of her heart, even from her nearest relations, felt ashamed to have shown her grief before a stranger.

It was a relief to her, however, to find that he had not the slightest idea who she was. From the conversation that followed, it appeared that he took her for a young governess, who was going abroad to earn her living, and she did not undeceive him, glad to preserve her incognito in this way ; it even cheered her to play the part. She had no difficulty in identifying herself with the poor governess, and with shy, downcast eyes

she received her travelling companion's advice
and comfort. In spite of her real grief, the
fantastic element in her was strong enough to
make her enjoy the mystification. When the
gentleman proposed that they should go out together and see the town through which they had
to pass, she consented, and spent two days there
in his company, after which they separated without having told each other their names or posi-
tions.

This little episode is very characteristic of
Sonia's taste for adventure. She liked the
stranger, his kind sympathy touched her ; why
not accept this little pleasure which chance
threw in her path? Another woman no doubt
would have been compromised in the eyes of the
gentleman by allowing herself such liberty ;
but to Sonia, who for so many years had lived
in companionship with her own husband without belonging to him, the affair seemed very
simple, and she was well aware that, in her intercourse with men, it lay with herself to draw the
· limit where she liked. No man could ever misunderstand her in this respect.

Later on, during her residence in Paris, she
showed a similar disregard of conventionality in
carrying to the extreme limit a relation, which

must needs have appeared suspicious to her hostess, who did not know what to think of her lodger on seeing a man come out of her room about two o'clock in the morning and climb over the garden-wall—the more so as this young man spent whole days with Sonia, and always remained late. Moreover, he was the only person with whom she had any intercourse. Very naturally, this looked suspicious ; yet the relation in this case was as platonic as could be imagined.

The young man was a Pole and a revolutionary, a mathematician and a poet.

His soul and hers were like two flames burning in unison ; nobody had ever understood her as he did—every mood, thought, and dream. They were continually together, and during their short hours of separation they wrote long epistles to one another. They wrote poems in company, and had even commenced writing a long romantic novel.

They were enthusiastic believers in the idea that human beings are created as pairs, so that each man or woman forms only one half of the complete creature, the other half existing somewhere on the globe, though only a rare and happy chance would join the two

in this life; in most cases they would only
find one another in their future existence.
Could anything be more romantic?

These two could not be united here on earth,
because the conditions for such an union had
already been spoilt. Even if Sonia could have
recovered her liberty, she had belonged to
another, and the young man, who had kept pure
for the sake of the woman who was to have been
his only love, could not reconcile himself to this
idea. Nor did she feel that she had a right to
belong to anybody else, for the bond that united
her to her husband was not entirely broken.
Now and then they wrote to each other, and
spoke of meeting again; and in her heart she had
a kindly feeling for him still.

So her relations to the Pole consisted exclusively of an exchange of thoughts, and an
abstract analysis of feelings.

They would sit together talking incessantly,
intoxicating themselves with a never-ending flow
of words, a special characteristic of the Slavonic
race.

For a time all this made Sonia forget the dis-
cordances of her real life—when suddenly fate
struck her with a brutal, crushing blow.

Her husband had lacked courage to survive

E

the discovery that he had been deceived into a scandalous fraud, and ruined his family. This highly gifted and distinguished man, so simple and unassuming in his manners, who never coveted for himself any of the amusements that money can procure, had fallen a victim to a swindle, which was quite contrary to his whole character and disposition.

This news threw Sonia on her bed with a violent nervous fever, from which she rose as if the nerve of her life had been cut asunder. Remorse at having left her husband, instead of remaining with him and supporting him,—though this would have been to condemn herself to an almost unendurable struggle,—tormented her with all the bitterness of the irreparable. During this illness and mental struggle her appearance had lost its freshness, she had become many years older, her fine complexion was gone, and a deep wrinkle had settled between her brows, where it remained ever after.

VI

THE FIRST INVITATION FROM SWEDEN

DURING her residence in St Petersburg, in 1876, Sonia had already made an acquaintance which was to be of decisive influence on her future.

Professor Mittag Leffler, a pupil of Weierstrass, like herself, had so frequently heard the professor speak of her remarkable ability, that he wished to make her acquaintance, and therefore paid her a visit.

This time no foreboding told Sonia how important this new acquaintance would become to her. She felt rather disinclined to receive the visit, because at that time she had quite laid aside her scientific studies, and did not even keep up her correspondence with her old master. But during her conversation with Mittag Leffler her former interest revived, and she revealed such acuteness of thought, such quickness of perception in the most intricate mathematical questions, that her visitor felt almost bewildered, when he looked at the youthful face before him. The impression he had received of her distinction as a female thinker was so deep, that several years later, when he was called to the professorship of mathematics at the recently-founded Stockholm University, one of his first steps was to send in a petition that Madame Kovalevsky might be nominated lecturer under him.

A few years before the death of her husband, Sonia had expressed a wish to obtain a situation as lecturer at some university. Mittag Leffler, warmly interested in the new centre of scientific study in his native town, as well as in the woman-question, eagerly desired to shed glory on the new university, by attaching to it the first really great female name in his science.

Already in 1881, with regard to these prospects, Sonia had written the following lines to Mittag Leffler :—

'Berlin, Bellevuestrasse,
'*July 8th*, 1881.

'. . . Nevertheless, I thank you most heartily for your wish that I may be called to Stockholm, and for all your efforts in the matter. As for myself, I can assure you that if the post of lecturer were offered me, I should be very glad to accept it. I have never aspired to anything higher, and I even confess to you, that to begin with I should feel less shy in this position, and quite satisfied to have an opportunity of employing my knowledge in the service of the higher education, and securing access for women to a university career, a privilege which hitherto has been bestowed only as an exception and a special favour, and might be easily and voluntarily withdrawn, as has been the case at most of the German universities.

'Without being rich, my means allow me to live quite independently, so that the question of salary would be irrelevant in this case. What I wish above all, is to serve a cause dear to me, and, at the same time, to work surrounded by persons who are occupied with the same studies as myself, an advantage I have always been longing for, which I miss in Russia, and which hitherto I have enjoyed only in Berlin.

'These, my dear Professor, are my personal feelings. But I must add another consideration. So far as Professor Weierstrass can judge of circumstances in Stockholm, he does not think that the university will ever admit a woman

among its teachers ; and, what is more important
still, he is afraid that your insisting on this innovation might prejudice your own position.   It
would be much too selfish on my part not to
inform you of our dear master's opinion on this
matter ; and you may imagine how sorry I should
be, if, after all, I became a hindrance to you,
who have always given me so much interest
and ready help, and for whom I feel the sincerest
friendship.

'Therefore, I think the wisest plan would be
not to take any step at present in this affair ;
to wait at any rate till I have finished the work
which occupies me just now.   If I succeed in my
task as well as I wish and hope, it will, at all
events, be a great help to me in reaching the end
I have in view.'

The succeeding dramatic events in Sonia's
life (separation from her husband, her romantic
episode with her Polish friend, Kovalevsky's
death, her own long illness), retarded the accom-
plishment of this task.   Not until August 1883
did she inform Mittag Leffler that she had
finished one of her books.   On August 28th,
she writes from Odessa :—

'At last I have brought to a close one of the

two works that have occupied my mind these two years. As soon as I thought I had obtained a satisfactory result, my first wish was to inform you of it; but Herr Weierstrass, with his usual kindness, undertook to write to you about my successful researches. I have just received a letter from him, telling me that he had written to you, and received your answer in return, in which, with your invariable kindness towards me, you ask me to come to Stockholm as soon as possible, in order to begin a course of private lectures there. I cannot sufficiently express my gratitude for the friendship you have always shewn me, nor tell you how happy I am to enter upon a career, which has been the object of my constant desires. Nevertheless, I must not conceal from you, that in many respects I do not feel myself qualified for the duties of a lecturer, and I am almost afraid that, in spite of your kind predilection for me, you will be quite disappointed with my performances, when you come to see them at close quarters.

'I feel so deeply obliged to the Stockholm University, which, alone among all, is willing to open its doors to me, that I can only wish to attach myself to Stockholm and Sweden, and to look upon them as my second country, hoping to remain there for many years. But for that very reason I should not like to go, until I feel I deserve your good opinion, and am able to create a favourable impression. I have written to Weierstrass to-day, asking whether he does not think it wiser for me to remain with him for two or three months more, in order to possess myself more thoroughly of his ideas, and to fill up the blanks which may still be left in my knowledge of mathematics.

'These two months in Berlin would also be of great advantage to me, in helping me to get into touch with the young mathematicians who are finishing their studies, or beginning their career as lecturers, and with whom I used to be closely connected during my last visit to Berlin. I might even arrange to exchange lessons with some of them, and undertake myself to expound the theory of the transformations of the Abel-functions, which they do not know, and which I have studied thoroughly. This would offer me an opportunity of lecturing, which, hitherto, I have not had at all, and I should come to Stockholm in January much more sure of myself.'

VII

ARRIVAL IN STOCKHOLM. FIRST IMPRESSIONS.

VERY naturally, my first meeting with Sonia stands engraved in my memory, especially since her death, in its minutest details. She had arrived by steamer from Finland the previous night, and was staying as guest in the house of my brother, Mittag Leffler. I went to call upon her in the morning.

We were prepared to become friends; having heard so much of each other, we were both longing to meet. Perhaps she had anticipated more pleasure from our acquaintance than I, for she took great interest in my vocation, whilst I was a little afraid that a mathematical woman would be too abstract for my taste.

When I entered she was standing near the library window with a book in her hand. Before she turned round, I had time to notice her grave profile, with somewhat large features, rich chestnut hair, rather carelessly coiled in a knot, a slender though not well-proportioned figure, the body appearing too small for the massive head. Her mouth was large, with full fresh lips, and very expressive in its distinctly marked lines. Her hands were very small, like a child's, and refined, though a little marred by two distinct blue veins.

But her eyes! They were of a wonderful expression, and gave to her face the peculiar charm that attracted everybody; their colour could not be defined, as it alternated between grey-green and brown; they sparkled with intelligence, as if piercing your soul to its innermost recesses. But at the same time they were kind and genial, beaming with sympathy, and, as with a kind of magnetic spell, won your confidence immediately. They were unusually large and convex; at times, when they were tired, you noticed a certain cast in them, which might be partly owing to their extreme short-sightedness.

She turned round quickly and met me with outstretched hands, yet there was a certain shyness in her manner, and her greeting was rather conventional. She told me that she had caught a violent toothache on the steamer, and I offered to take her to a dentist—rather an unpleasant beginning in her new home.

At that time my mind was taken up with the plan of a play, 'How we do good,' but I had written nothing of it as yet. So great was her power of drawing others out, that before we arrived at the dentist's, I had told her the whole thing much more completely than I had seen it myself before. And ever afterwards she continued to exercise the greatest influence on all I wrote. She had an extraordinary gift of understanding and sympathising ; her approval was so warm and enthusiastic, her censure so scorching, that it became impossible to a receptive nature like mine to work without her approval. If she happened to blame anything I had written, I kept changing it till she was pleased—and this was the beginning of our collaboration. She used to say that I should never have written 'True Women'* if I had known her before it was published, for this play as well as 'War against Society,' were the only works of mine which she disliked. 'True Women' for a

* Translated into English by Mr H. L. Brækstad, and published by Samuel French, Strand.

very characteristic reason : she blamed Bertha's struggle to save the remainder of her fortune for her mother's sake, ' for,' said she, ' when a woman has given herself to a man, she must not hesitate to sacrifice her fortune to him to the last penny.'

This criticism was just like her, for she was in the highest degree individual in her judgment of literary matters. If the thoughts and sentiments of the work agreed with her own, she felt inclined to praise it, though it might be of small literary value. On the other hand, if the author shocked her by his views, she would scarcely admit any merit in his production.

In spite of these prejudices, her views on life were very large, such as we find only in the most superior minds of our time. She was perfectly free from conventional and commonplace opinions. Her strong dash of genius, and her wide culture, raised her high over the narrow horizon within which traditional views keep most minds prisoned. Her only limitations were those of her strong sympathies and antipathies, which braved all logic and argument.

Our intercourse this first time did not last long, and did not as yet develop into intimate friendship, because I started on a long journey abroad a few months after her arrival. However, before we parted, she had learned Swedish enough to read all my works. Immediately after her arrival she began to learn the language, and kept studying it from morning till night for several weeks. When my brother said to her that he was going to give a party to his scientific friends, in order to introduce them to her, she answered, 'Wait a fortnight, till I can speak Swedish.'

This seemed rather bold, but she kept her word. At the appointed time she could speak a little, and already during the first winter she acquainted herself with our whole modern literature, and read 'Frithiof's Saga' with delight.

This extraordinary talent for languages, however, had its limitations. She used to say herself, that she had no particular gift that way, and that it was only ambition and necessity that made her learn them so quickly. And indeed, though she learned many languages, she never acquired perfection in any, but always stopped at a certain point. Though she was very young when she went to Germany, she spoke very broken German, and her friends often laughed at the funny words she concocted. In her flow of eloquence she never stopped to choose the most correct expression, and she forgot quickly. After having learned Swedish she nearly forgot her German, and after a few months' absence from Sweden her Swedish used to be miserable. Moreover, with language as with everything else, much depended on her personal mood. When tired and indisposed she had difficulty in finding words, but when in high spirits she expressed herself with ease and elegance.

She often regretted that she could not speak Russian with her intimate friends in Sweden, as it prevented her from expressing the most delicate shades of her thoughts. In Russia it was as if she had escaped from a kind of prison, where her best thoughts had been kept under lock and key. At the same time her country-men censured her style, because of certain foreign elements in it.

In February 1884, I went to London, and did not see Sonia again till September the same year. I received only one letter from her, in which she gives the following description of her first winter in Stockholm :—

' What shall I tell you about our life in Stock-holm ? Though not very eventful, it has been animated enough, and of late rather fatiguing.

Suppers, dinners, soirées continually. It was
rather difficult to attend all, and yet find time
for preparing lectures. We stopped to-day for
a fortnight's Easter holidays, and I am as glad
as a schoolgirl. The term will soon be at an
end, and then I hope to go to Berlin by St
Petersburg. My plans for the next winter, of
course, are unsettled, they do not depend upon
myself.

'As you may imagine, everybody talks of
you, and wants to hear about you. Your letters
are read and commended ; they create a regular
sensation. The leading ladies of Stockholm
seem to lack interesting and exciting subjects of
conversation, and it is a charity to provide them
with such matter. I am looking forward to and
at the same time trembling for the fate of your
play.'

In April, Sonia brought her course of lectures
to a close, and went to Russia. She writes
from there to Mittag Leffler :—

'April 29th, 1884.

'. . . It appears a century since I left Stockholm. I shall never in my life be able to show
or tell you my gratitude and friendship for you.
It seems that I have found a new home-country

and a new family in Sweden at the very moment when I was most in need of it. . . .'

The lectures which Sonia had delivered at the University that winter—in German—had been of an entirely private nature, but they had been so highly appreciated that it became possible to Mittag Leffler privately to collect the means necessary to secure her appointment to the professorship for five years. A number of private persons undertook to contribute 2000 kroner a year (about £111), the University added a similar sum, so that a salary of £222 was offered to Sonia.

Her pecuniary situation no longer allowed her to do the work for nothing, as she had been liberal enough to offer at first. But it was not the financial question which caused difficulties.

There was opposition to overcome which arose from many sides against the admission of women to the post of professors in the University. The case was unprecedented, as no other University in the world had granted this privilege as yet. At the end of the five years, however, Mittag Leffler succeeded in his efforts: Sonia was nominated for life. (Only a year later death put a sudden end to her career).

On the 1st of July 1884, Mittag Leffler had
the pleasure of telegraphing to Sonia, who was
in Berlin at that time, that she had been called
to the professorship for five years. She answered
the same day as follows :—

'BERLIN, *July 1st*, 1884.

'. . . I need not tell you the joy it gave me to
receive your telegram and Uggla's. I may confess now, that up to the last moment I did not
believe that the thing would come to pass. I
kept fearing that some unforeseen difficulty would
turn up, as so frequently happens in this life, and
that all our plans would finally collapse. And,
indeed, I have not the slightest doubt that my
success in this matter is due only to your perseverance and energy. I now wish, with all my
heart, that I may have sufficient strength and
capacity to do my duties to the utmost, and to
support you well in all your enterprises. I trust
firmly in the future, and I am happy at the prospect of working with you. What a chance that
we have met one another in life. . . . ;' and in
the same letter, . . . ' Weierstrass has spoken to
several persons in the university with regard to
my wish of attending lectures here. There is
some hope that the matter may be arranged, but

not this summer, for the present Rector is an ardent reactionary on the woman question. I hope I shall succeed in obtaining admission in December, when I shall be back here for my holidays. . . .'

We see that while the Stockholm University had already accepted Madame Kovalevsky as professor, the mere fact of her sex still excluded her from even hearing university lectures in the German capital.

Anybody else no doubt would have felt some uneasiness at the uncertainty of the position she now accepted ; but Sonia never was anxious about the future. If the present satisfied her she did not claim any more, and at any time she would have been ready to sacrifice a glorious future, if for that price she could have bought happiness for the time being.

Before going to Berlin that summer Sonia had visited her daughter, who was staying with a friend in Moscow. From there she wrote to Mittag Leffler in a way which explains her views regarding her maternal duties, and the conflict between her obligations as a mother and as a public person.

'Moskow, *June* 3*rd*, 1884.

'. . . I have received a long letter from T., in

which she insists on my taking my child with
me to Stockholm ; but in spite of all the reasons
that might make me wish to live with my little
girl, I have almost made up my mind to leave
her in Moscow.   I do not think it would be to
her interest to take her away from this house
where she is so comfortable.   In Stockholm no
house is ready to receive her, and I shall be
obliged to devote all my time and energy to my
new duties.   She mentions among other reasons,
that many persons will accuse me of indifference
towards my daughter ; very likely, but I confess
this reason has no value in my eyes.   I am ready
to submit to the judgment of Stockholm ladies
in all small matters of life, but in serious questions, where not only my own but my child's
welfare is concerned, I think it would be an un-
pardonable weakness to be influenced even by
the shadow of a wish to appear a good mother
in those ladies' eyes.'

After her return to Sweden in September, Sonia
settled down for a time in Soedertelje, in order
to find undisturbed leisure to finish an important
work she had commenced many years previously, upon the refraction of light in a crystal-
line medium.   Mittag Leffler and a young

German mathematician, with whom Sonia had made acquaintance in Berlin, were also staying there; the latter helped her with the German edition of her work.

On visiting her there after my return from abroad, I was struck by finding her look younger and prettier than before. First I thought it was because she had left off mourning, for black did not suit her at all, and she hated wearing it. The light blue dress set off her complexion to great advantage, and she had curled her rich chestnut hair.

But the change was not outward only. I even noticed that her sadness had given way to the overflowing gaiety which was the other side of her character, and which I saw for the first time now. During these periods she was exuberant with life and spirit; half sarcastic, half good-natured jokes were showering down constantly; she would fling out the boldest paradoxes, and if you were not quick of retort you had better hold your tongue on those occasions, for she did not leave you time for reflection.

At the same time she was preparing her lectures for the next term, which she delivered before the young German, whom she called her experimental rabbit (Versuchskaninchen), a part which, as a rule, had fallen to the share of Mittag Leffler.

Her high spirits continued during the autumn; she went much into society, and everywhere formed the centre of a large circle.

There was a strong sarcastic element in Sonia's nature; she was a worshipper of genius and intelligence, and despised mediocrity. But, at the same time, she was endowed with the poet's understanding and sympathetic feeling for all life's conflicts, even the most insignificant. She listened with encouraging interest to all her friends' concerns, whether household troubles or questions of dress, etc., etc.

It was frequently said that she was as simple and unassuming as a school girl, not thinking herself superior to any other woman; but this was a mistake. Her openness was only apparent, in reality she was very reserved; but the elasticity of her manners and of her intelligence, her desire to please, and her psychological interest for all that was human, gave her the sympathetic appearance which attracted everybody. She very rarely vented her sarcasm on persons inferior to herself, unless she disliked them very much, but she gave it free play with those whom she considered her equals.

However, she had soon exhausted society life in Stockholm ; after a very short time she declared that she knew everybody by heart, and she began to long for new excitements. It was her misfortune that she could never feel contented in Stockholm, and perhaps nowhere in the world ; that she constantly wanted stimulus for her mind. Everyday life, with its grey monotony, was hateful to her ; she was a gipsy-nature, as she used to say herself, and did not feel capable of cultivating civic virtues.

She attributed this peculiar temper to her descent from a gipsy girl, whom her great grand-father had married. It was a characteristic of her intelligence as well ; she was of a very recep-tive, as well as highly productive, nature, and required stimulation from the genius of others, in order to produce something herself. Her scientific work, indeed, was only a development of her great master's ideas.

And in her literary productions, too, she absolutely needed exchange of ideas with others who were occupied with the same kind of work. In fact, life in a small town like Stockholm was too stagnating for her ; she could only thrive in large European capitals.

This year—1884—she spent Christmas in

Berlin, and it was on her return from that visit that I first heard her utter the sentence, which afterwards she repeated every year, and which pained and wounded her friends: 'The way from Stockholm to Malmö appears to me one of the finest railway lines I have ever seen ; but the way from Malmö to Stockholm, the ugliest, slowest, dreariest journey I know.'

My heart shrinks when I think how often she had to make that journey with ever increasing bitterness, till at last it led her to her grave.

A letter to my brother that Christmas shows how deeply melancholy her general disposition was, in spite of all outward gaiety. Her friends relate that during this visit to Berlin she was more cheerful than they had ever seen her. She regretted that in her youth she had neglected all entertainments usually enjoyed by young people, and now she was going to have compensation So she began to take lessons in dancing and skating. As she did not wish to exhibit her first attempts on the ice in a public place, one of her friends and admirers arranged a private skating corner for her in his own garden in a modern suburb of Berlin. The dancing lessons went on in the same way, in a private room, with a few admirers as partners. She hurried on from one pleasure to another, and was much courted, which always pleased her.

But this cheerfulness did not last long. After a month, it was already succeeded by melancholia, caused partly by the news of her sister's illness, partly by a little love affair, which, as usual, turned out unhappily for her. This lay really at the bottom of her high spirits, as well as of her depression.

On December 27th, she writes :—

'I am very low, for I have received bad news from my sister ; her illness makes awful progress. Now her sight is affected ; she can neither read nor write. It all comes from the same source—weakness of the heart, which causes partial congestion of blood and paralysis. It makes me tremble to think of the awful loss that may be in store for me in the near future. How horrid life is, and how stupid it is to continue to live. To-day is my birthday, I am thirty-one,* and it is dreadful to think that I may have to live perhaps as many years more.

'In plays and novels, things are arranged much more conveniently ; if a person finds that life has lost its value to him, somebody or something turns up that helps him to pass quickly over

---

* She was two or three years older.

the border into another world. In this respect, reality is very inferior to fiction. There is so much talk about the organic perfection which the living creatures have gradually developed in themselves by natural selection, etc. I really think the most desirable perfection would be the gift of dying quickly and easily. Evidently man has degenerated. Insects and animals of lower order can never make up their minds to die ; it is appalling how much an infusory can suffer, without ceasing to live. But the higher you ascend through the scale of living creatures, the easier and quicker you will find the transition. For a bird, a wild beast, lion or tiger, almost every illness is mortal ; either full enjoyment of life, or death—no suffering. But the highest creature, man, again resembles the insect on this point: their wings may be torn off, their limbs crushed, legs broken, etc., and yet they do not die !

'Pardon me for writing so sadly to you to-day; I am in a very black mood, and what is worse I feel no desire for work. I have not had the energy to begin preparing my lectures for the next term, though I have been dreaming a good deal about the following problem' (here follows a mathematical question).

I shall quote one more passage from the same letter :—

'Your sister sent me as a Christmas gift, an article by Strindberg, in which he proves, as clearly as twice two make four, that a female professor of mathematics is a monstrous thing, a nuisance, most unpleasant and unprofitable. After all, I think he is right; I only protest against the idea that Sweden possesses a large number of mathematicians superior to myself, and that I have only been elected from motives of gallantry.'

VIII

SPORTS AND OTHER PASTIMES

AMONG the skaters who crowded on Nybrovike
and the royal skating place on Sheppsholm
the following winter, you might have seen a
little lady in a tight-fitting, fur-trimmed mantle;
she was short-sighted, held her hand in her
muff, and advanced carefully on her skates by
the side of a tall gentleman with spectacles,
and an equally tall, thin lady, who did not
skate very well either. They always talked
eagerly, and sometimes the gentleman would
draw mathematical figures on the ice—not with
his skates—he did not master the art sufficiently
for that—but with his walking stick, and the
small lady would stop, and look on attentively.
They came from the University, where one of
them had been lecturing, and some scientific
question had caused an eager discussion, which
continued while they were skating. Now and

then the lady would give a little shriek, and
ask to be spared mathematics on the ice, because
it made her lose her balance.   Or the two ladies
would exchange psychological observations, or
tell one another their plans for novels or plays.
Sometimes they would quarrel about their skill
in skating, and willing as they were otherwise
to acknowledge one another's merits, in this case
alone, neither would ever give precedence to the
other.   In fact, Sonia seemed prouder of every
little progress she made in skating, than of her
scientific triumphs.

The two ladies would even sometimes appear
at the riding school.   Of course everybody
noticed the famous Madame Kovalevsky where-
ever she appeared ; but one could not help
wondering at her childish behaviour on these
occasions.   Though she seemed to take great
interest in riding, she had not the slightest turn
for it.   She lost her self-control on horseback,
screaming loudly as soon as the horse made the
slightest unexpected movement ; and though she
always got the quietest horse that was to be
had, it was the animal's fault, not her own, if
she did not ride well—it had been restive, or
jolted, etc.   To trot for ten minutes at a time,
was all she ever could accomplish, and often,

when the horse had just started, she would call out breathlessly in her broken Swedish :—'Dear Mr N. N. *do* stop him!'

However, anybody who did not know this, would think her a great rider, from the way she talked about her horsemanship.

In a letter to a friend and admirer in Berlin, who had taught her dancing and skating, Sonia describes her life in Stockholm in the winter of 1885 :—

'Dear Mr W., I feel very guilty not to have answered your kind letter before. My only excuse is, that my time has been taken up of late by the most heterogeneous occupations. I shall tell you what I have been doing.

'First of all, I have to prepare three weekly lectures in Swedish ; I am lecturing about the algebraic introductions to the theory of the Abel-functions, which everywhere in Germany are considered the most difficult subjects. I have a large attendance, and till now have kept all my hearers ; only two or three have fallen off.

'2. I have written a little mathematical essay, which I am going to send to Weierstrass, asking him to have it published in Borchardt's Journal.

'3. Mittag Leffler and I have commenced a very important mathematical work, from which we anticipate great satisfaction and success. However, this is a secret, and you will please not mention it.

'4. I have made the acquaintance of a very amiable person, who has just arrived from America, and who is now the editor of the greatest Swedish paper. He has persuaded me to contribute to it, and as I cannot see any of my friends do a thing without being tempted to do the same (which you have probably noticed), I have written some short articles for him. At present, only one of them has appeared in print, and I send it to you, as you know Swedish well enough to understand it.

'5. (Last, not least.) Can you imagine— improbable as it may appear—I have become quite a clever skater. Till the end of last week I have been practising almost every day. I am very sorry that you will have no opportunity of seeing how well I skate now. At every step of progress I thought of you. I can even skate backward quite easily. My friends here are surprised to see how quickly I have learned this difficult art.

' Now that the ice is gone, and I have begun to ride, my friend and I enjoy it very much. During our Easter holidays, we mean to ride

an hour daily at least. I don't know which
I prefer, riding or skating.

'But this is not all. On the 15th of April,
we are to have a great public festival—a genuine
Swedish entertainment, it seems—a kind of
bazaar. A hundred ladies are to appear in
different costumes, and to sell a variety of things,
in order to provide funds for building a National
Museum. I am to be a gipsy of course. Five
young ladies are to join me in a band, and
we are to have a tent with five young men
to help us.

'What do you think of my frivolity, dear
Mr W.? This evening I am to have a party
in my own little home, for the first time in
Stockholm.'

In spring the same year, the question arose of
appointing Sonia as Professor *ad interim* of
Mechanical Philosophy, during the severe illness
of Professor Holmgren.

In June, Madame Kovalevsky started for
Russia, where she meant to spend part of the
summer in St Petersburg with her suffering sister, part of it in Moscow and its
neighbourhood with her friend and her little
daughter.

I was in Switzerland with my brother, and

we had asked her to meet us there. She
answered as follows :—

'MY DEAREST ANN CHARLOTTE,—I have
just received your kind letter. You cannot
imagine how I should like to start at once and
meet you in Switzerland, and how I should
enjoy climbing the Alps with you. I quite
realise the pleasure it would have been, and
what happy weeks we might have spent together.
Unfortunately, many reasons retain me here, one
more stupid than the other. First of all, I have
promised to stay till the 1st of August, and
though it is my principle that man is above his
word, old prejudices are so strong with me that
I always hesitate to carry out my theories ; so,
instead of being the mistress, I become the
slave of my word.

'. . . Your brother, who indeed knows and
judges me very well (though we must not tell him
so, as it would flatter his vanity too much), has
often said that I am very impressionable, and
that I am always guided by the impulse of the
moment. In Stockholm, where I am looked
upon as a champion of women's rights, I
usually think that it is my greatest and absolute
duty to cultivate my genius. But I humbly

confess that here, being introduced to every new acquaintance as " Faufi's Mamma" is so great a blow to my vanity, that it calls forth an abundance of feminine virtues of which you would never think me capable.

'All these influences, which at present rule your poor friend, are strong enough to keep me back here, at least till the 15th of August. The only thing I may hope to do is to meet you in Normandy, and to go to Aberdeen with your brother. Write soon to me, dear kind Ann Charlotte. How happy you are, and how I envy you.

'I shall do what I can to meet you in Normandy.—Bien à toi !

'SONIA.'

Sonia's plans of going to Normandy and Scotland came to nothing. She remained the whole summer in Russia, and we did not meet again till September in Stockholm.

Part of a letter from Madame Kovalevsky to her friend Mr W., in Berlin :—

'. . . I am living with my friend, Julia L., at a small property of hers near Moscow. I have found my daughter cheerful and in good health.

G

I cannot tell which of us, mother or child, was the happier when we met again. Now we shall not part, at least not for some time to come, for in the autumn she is to join me in Stockholm. She will soon be six years old, and is a sensible little girl for her age. People say she resembles me very much, and I fancy I looked like her when I was a child. My friend is very depressed, as she has just lost her only sister. Therefore our home is very quiet and sad. We are surrounded by ladies, four old maids; as they all wear deep mourning, the house seems like a nunnery. As in a convent, eating is a very important business here : four times a day, tea with cakes, sweets, sugared fruits, etc., which helps to kill the time. However, I try to bring a little change into this monotony, so to-day I persuaded Julia to take a drive with me, all by ourselves. I assured her that I could drive perfectly well, so the coachman was left at home. And indeed we arrived all right at our destination, but on our way home the horse shied, the carriage was flung against a tree, and we fell into the ditch.

'Poor Julia hurt her foot badly, and I, the guilty person, escaped unhurt from the adventure. . . .'

IX

VARYING MOODS

DURING the following winter the sentimental element became prominent in Sonia's inner life. She found nothing more to attract her in society; her thoughts were not absorbed by much work; her lectures did not interest her particularly, and under such circumstances she was always given to dark moods; she would brood over her fate, and grieve that life had not offered her what she wanted beyond everything.

She no longer insisted upon her former idea, that humanity was divided into two exact halves, and that one love only ought to be decisive for our whole life. She raved about a union between man and wife, in which the intelligence of each supplemented that of the other, so that co-operation between the two should be necessary for producing the ripe fruit of their genius. It was her great object to realise this ideal for herself, and she dreamt of finding the man who, in this sense, might become her second self. The thought that she would never meet this man in Sweden, made her feel a certain discontent with this country, to which she had come with such bright hopes and anticipations.

Mathematician as she was, the aim and end of life could not be found in abstract science by a character like hers, which was so passionately personal in all its tendencies.

When she argued about these ideas with Mittag Leffler, he used to call them an outcome of feminine weakness, and to say that a genius was never to such an extent dependent on others. However, she insisted and quoted many men who had found their highest aspirations in their love for one woman. It is true, most of these men were poets, and it was rather difficult to find examples among men of science; yet, Sonia was never at a loss for proofs; where facts were wanting her imagination would come to the rescue, and she certainly showed how the sense of solitude had been the greatest trial to all deep natures, and how man, whose highest dream of happiness was to live in fullest intimate harmony with another being, always in his innermost self was doomed to solitude.

I remember particularly the spring of 1886. Spring-time was always trying to Sonia; this season of fermentation, growth, and restlessness used to oppress her, make her nervous, impatient, and over-sensitive. The long days enervated her, while I used to love them. The constant light, she used to say, seems to promise so much, and yet to give so little, because the earth remains cold. Summer vanishes quickly like a phantom, you cannot keep it in your grasp. She could not work, and kept insisting that work in itself, especially scientific production, had no value, could give no joy, nor yet promote the happiness of men. It was folly to lose one's youth in work; it was a misfortune, especially for a woman, to have a natural gift for science, as it would draw her into a sphere where she could never find happiness.

As soon as her term in Stockholm was over she hurried abroad, and went first to Paris, where she wrote me one single letter. Contrary to her habit, it was dated.

'142 BOULEVARD DE L'ENFER,
'*June 26th*, 1886.

'DEAR ANN CHARLOTTE,—I have this moment received your letter. I blame myself

dreadfully for not having written before. I am
quite willing to confess that I was a little jealous,
and that I thought you did not care for me at
all. As I wish my letter to start to-day, I
can only write a few lines to tell you that you
are very wrong in supposing that I forget you
when I am away. Perhaps I have never realised
as I do at present, how fond I am of you and
your brother. At every pleasure I enjoy, my
thoughts naturally turn to you. I am enjoying
myself very much here, for all the mathematicians make a great fuss about me; still I am
longing for a wicked brother and sister, who
have become quite indispensable to my life. I
cannot leave Paris till July the 5th, so I cannot
be in Christiania for the opening of the Naturalists' Congress. Can you wait for me (in
Copenhagen), so that we may go together ?
Please answer immediately. I have given your
book to Jonas Lie ; he speaks of you with much
friendship. When he called he had not yet
read your book. He thinks you have more
talent for novel-writing than for the drama. I
shall see him once more before leaving. I embrace you tenderly, and am longing to see you
again, my dear dear Ann Charlotte.—Ever yours,

'SONIA.'

As usual, she could not tear herself away from Paris till the last moment, so that she only arrived in Christiania on the last day of the naturalists' meeting. I was accustomed to violent ups and downs in her moods, but this time the contrast was very striking between her spirits now and her depressed humour during the first months of the year, and particularly during the previous spring in Stockholm. She had lived much with Poincaré and other great mathematicians in Paris, and this intercourse had revived her energy for work, and encouraged her to try the solution of the problem which was to create her greatest fame, and procure her the first prize from the French Academy of Science.

And now science had become the only thing in the world worth living for; everything else— personal happiness, love, nature—was worthless; search for scientific truth was the most beautiful object in life, and exchange of ideas with your equals, without personal tie, was the most glorious thing in the world.

The creative spirit was over her, and she had again one of her brilliant periods, when she was all beauty, genius, sparkling life.

She arrived in Christiania at night, after three days' voyage from Hâvre. She had suffered awfully from sea-sickness the whole time, but untiring as she was when her spirits were up, next morning, after a few hours' sleep, she was ready to start on an excursion and to attend a festival, which went on till late the following night.

Many speeches were made in her honour on this occasion, and all the most distinguished persons crowded round her. On this day, as usual under similar circumstances, she was so amiable, modest, and gentle, that she won all hearts.

From Christiania we travelled some days together through Thelemarken, where we visited Ullman's Popular High School, for which Sonia showed warm interest. This visit gave her the first impulse for a series of articles about these peculiar Scandinavian high schools, which she sent to a Russian periodical, and which proved such a success that the number of subscribers to the paper increased considerably.

From Siljord we started on foot, and climbed one of the mountains ; probably the first expedition of this kind Sonia had ever made. She was bold, quick, and untiring, delighted with the scenery, full of joy and life. She was fond of Nature in her own way ; she felt the charm and

poetry in a landscape. But her sight was very
short, and she did not wear spectacles, partly
from feminine coquetry, and partly from fear of
looking like the traditional blue stocking, and so
could not take in the details of the surrounding
Nature. If, nevertheless, in some of her works
we find not only very fine pictures of landscape,
its general impression, its soul, so to say, but
also a true rendering of its details, this was owing,
no doubt, more to abstract knowledge than to
personal observation. She was well grounded in
natural history, had helped her husband in trans-
lating Brehm's 'Birds,' and had shared his
studies of palæontology and geology. She had
also had much personal intercourse with the
most distinguished contemporary naturalists.
But, after all, her taste depended very much
on her mood. When in good spirits, the most
uninteresting landscape became beautiful in her
eyes, and when out of humour she was perfectly
indifferent to the finest effects of colour and line.
On the whole, she lacked a just eye for pure
symmetrical form, for harmony, proportion,
colour, and other objective phases of beauty.
Thus, if a person was sympathetic to her, or
possessed some of the qualities she particularly admired, she would consider him or

her good-looking, while others were ugly who might not deserve this qualification. As a rule she admired fair people, seldom dark ones.

I cannot help mentioning here that she lacked all sense of art in a remarkable degree, quite astonishing in a person of her extraordinary cleverness. She had spent years in Paris without once visiting the Louvre; neither pictures, sculptures, nor architecture, ever attracted her attention.

However, she was highly charmed with Norwegian scenery, and liked the people as well. We had planned a long journey in Norway, and a visit to the poet Alexander Kielland; but though she had been looking forward to this for years, she changed her mind all of a sudden. The creative spirit had come over her, and she could not resist its powerful voice. We were just crossing one of the Norwegian lakes, when the idea seized her that she must set to work immediately; so she took leave of me, and went on board another steamer, which took her to Christiania, and from there to Sweden.

I could neither object nor blame her; still it was a great disappointment to me. I continued the journey with a chance companion, visited Kielland, returned eastward, and attended a festival at a popular high school. All this, no doubt, would have given Sonia as much pleasure as it gave me, if her mind had been disengaged.

I noticed these sudden changes in my friend more than once. She might be in the midst of the most lively conversation at a party or on a journey, apparently quite absorbed by her surroundings; when the working fit seized her she became quiet, her eyes wandered, her answers showed that her mind was absent; she would say good-bye, and no persuasion, no previous appointment, no regard for anything else, could induce her to remain.

We had agreed that I should join her later on, in the place where she had settled down, with my brother and his family. But I had scarcely arrived there, when Sonia was called away by a telegram to her sister in Russia, who had been seized by a new and severe attack of her illness.

When she came back, in September, she had her little daughter (now eight years old) with her, and for the first time she settled down in apartments of her own in Stockholm.

She was tired of living in a boarding-house. Though perfectly indifferent to home comforts, to food and to furniture, she had a great wish to be independent, and absolute mistress of her time; and she could not bear any longer to submit to the many restraints which are unavoidable when living with others. So, with the help of friends, she took apartments, and got a housekeeper, who was to take care of the child as well, bought some pieces of furniture, and sent for others from Russia. However, even this home bore the stamp of a temporary arrangement, ready to be broken up at any moment.

The drawing-room furniture, which had come from Russia, was quite characteristic. It was from her parents' house, and recalled all the pomp and splendour of an old mansion. It had filled a huge room, and consisted of: a sofa, which occupied the whole length of one wall, a corner sofa, deep arm-chairs, all of richly carved mahogany, and upholstered with scarlet silk damask; however, the stuff was torn here and there, the stuffing worn out, the springs partly broken. Sonia meant to have it all repaired, and the furniture re-covered; but this was never done, partly because, according to Russian ideas, ragged furniture was nothing extraordinary, partly because Sonia never felt really at home in Stockholm. To her it was only a station on a journey, and she did not care to spend anything on it.

Sometimes, when in good spirits, she would get a fit of energy, and amuse herself with decorating her rooms with her own hand-made embroideries. One day she sent me the following note :—

'ANN CHARLOTTE,—Last night you gave me a striking proof that critics are right in asserting that you have an open eye for what is bad and ugly, but not for what is good and fine. Every spot, every tear on one of my dear old chairs is sure to be discovered by you, though it may be ever so much hidden by antimacassars, but you did not even condescend to look once at my splendid new cover for the rocking-chair, which tried in vain the whole evening to attract your attention.—Yours,

'SONIA.'

X

WHAT WAS AND WHAT MIGHT HAVE BEEN.

SONIA had scarcely settled down in this rather peculiar home when she was called to Russia once more. In the middle of winter she had to go by steamer to Helsingfors (Finland), and thence by railway to St Petersburg, to her suffering sister, whose life was in imminent danger. On such occasions she knew no fear, and heeded no difficulties. She was devoted to her sister, and ready to make great sacrifices for her sake.

She left her daughter in my charge during her two months' absence.

I have kept but one letter of this period; it shows how sadly she spent her Christmas that year :—

'DEAR ANN CHARLOTTE,—I arrived here last night. I can only write a few lines to-day. My sister is dreadfully ill, though the doctor assures me that she is better than she was some days ago. Nothing can be more cruel than such long, painful, and consuming diseases! She suffers agonies, can neither sleep nor breathe properly. . . . I do not know how long I shall have to remain here. I am longing much for Faufi (her daughter) and my work. The journey was very troublesome and slow.—With fond love to you all, your devoted friend,

'SONIA.'

During the long days and nights she spent in this way beside her sister's sick-bed, she naturally brooded over many things. The thought struck her how things were and how they might have been. She remembered the golden dreams with which the two sisters had started in life, both young, good-looking, highly gifted, and it struck her how little life had brought them of the anticipated happiness, though it had been rich and eventful to both of them.

Still in the innermost recesses of their hearts there was a burning sensation of disappointed hopes.

How very different, Sonia said to herself, everything might have been, if they had not both made certain fatal mistakes.

Out of these reflections was born the idea of writing two parallel novels, which were to relate the history of the same person in two different ways. They were to be represented in the prime of youth, with all its possibilities, and led to an important crisis in life. One of the novels was to show the consequences of the choice they had actually made, the other how things might have turned out if they had chosen the reverse.

Who amongst us, Sonia reasoned, has not a false step to repent of, and who has not wished many a time to be able to live his life over again from the beginning? It was this wish, this dream, she wanted to give shape in a novel —if she had the gift of doing it, which seemed rather doubtful to her. So when she came home to Stockholm, full of enthusiasm for her new idea, she tried to persuade me that we should write it together.

Just about this time I had commenced a new

SOPHIE KOVALEVSKY.

1887.

novel entitled, " Outside Matrimony," which was
meant to be the history of unmarried women,
of all those who for various reasons had never
had an opportunity of founding their own
family. It was to describe their thoughts
about love and marriage, the interests that
filled their lives,—in short, it was to be the
romance of all those who, according to accepted
ideas, have no romance. I meant it to be a
kind of counterpart to Garborg's ' Men Folk,' in
which he gives a similar history of bachelor life.
I had collected a number of types of single
women amongst my contemporaries, and I was
very much taken up with .my subject. Then
Sonia came with her idea, and her influence
over me was so great that she soon succeeded·
in making me desert my own child and adopt
hers. Some letters which I wrote at the time
will show the enthusiasm which filled us both
for this work :—

' February 2nd, 1887.

' . . . . Sonia and I have conceived a
grand plan ; we are going to write a great drama
in ten acts—which is to be divided into two
parts, of which each will take an evening. The
idea is hers, but I am to work it out. It is a

H

most original idea, I think. One play is to describe how things were, the other how they might have been. In the first piece all are unhappy, because we generally impede one another's happpiness here in life ; in the second, the same characters appear living for and helping one another, forming a small communistic and ideal society, where all become happy. Don't mention this to anybody as yet. To tell the truth, I don't know much more than Sonia's idea; we talked about it yesterday for the first time, and to-morrow she is going to explain her plan in detail; then I shall see whether the subject lends itself to dramatic treatment. You will probably laugh at my having settled the whole affair already, but that is always my way. No sooner have I got hold of an idea, than it grows before my eyes, and I see the whole plan accomplished. So I imagine Sonia and myself co-operating in a gigantic work, which is to make its way over the whole globe, and become a wonderful success. We are quite foolish about it. If we succeed we shall be reconciled to everything. Sonia will forget that Sweden is the most petty, narrow-minded country on earth, she will cease to regret the loss of her best years here, and

I shall forget—well, all the things I grumble at. . . . Very likely you think we are a couple of children ; well, so we are. Fortunately, there is a region, better than all countries on earth, the realm of fancy, which is open to both of us, where everybody can reign supreme, where everything can be arranged according to our own desires. . . . It may be, after all, that Sonia's plan will not do for a drama ; she meant it for a novel, but I could not write one after somebody else's plan, as a novel requires much more exclusive relationship between the author and his work and the drama.'

And on February 10th :—

' Sonia is overflowing with happiness at what she calls this new event in her life. She says that now she can fully understand how a man keeps falling in love with the mother of his children. I, of course, am the mother, as it falls to my share to bring forth the children, and she is so fond of me that it makes me quite happy to see her radiant eyes resting upon me. We are as delighted with each other's company, as perhaps two female friends have never been— for we shall be the first example in literature of two female collaborators.

'. . . I have never worked so quickly; as a rule, an idea must keep growing in my mind for months before I begin writing.'

On the 9th of March we had the first reading of our work to a familiar circle. Up to this moment our pleasures and our illusions had been constantly increasing. I never remember having seen Sonia so beaming with delight.

But on hearing it read to others we were struck by all its faults and shortcomings, and our plays, which had been written in feverish haste, had now to pass through the ordeal of re-modelling.

During the whole winter Sonia was incapable of giving attention to her mathematical work; and yet the term of competition for the Prix Bordin had been fixed, and she ought to have devoted all her efforts to the task.

Mittag Leffler, who felt in a way responsible for her, and who thought it might be of great importance for her to win this prize, was in despair when every time he called he found her in her drawing-room working at a piece of embroidery. She had got a mania for this occupation; while her needle moved in and out mechanically, her thoughts worked apace, and scene after scene unrolled itself before her mental vision. It was quite a race betwixt her needle and my pen, and whenever we found that the two had arrived at the same result, our joy was so great, that it quite compensated for the conflicts that would arise on seeing that our fancy had led us in different directions.

During the second writing of the last play, I had to forbid Sonia to enter my study whilst I was at work. Our continued collaboration in the first part became too disturbing and exciting for me. I lost the general view of the whole and the intimate familiarity with my characters.

In spite of the affinity of our characters, Sonia and I are contrasts in our methods of working. She is like Alice (in ' The Struggle for Happiness '), who can create nothing, embrace nothing with her whole heart, unless she can find somebody to share it with her. All her mathemathical works have been produced under the influence of another person ; even her lectures are only delivered well when she knows that Mittag Leffler is present.

Sonia herself often jokingly acknowledged this dependence on her surroundings.

In Alice she describes her own character. In the great scene with Hjalmar (1st Play, Act iii.),

Alice says : ' Do let me show you for once what
I can be, when I feel that I am really loved.   I
do not think that I am quite without attraction.
Look at me, am I beautiful?   Yes, if you
love me, I am—not otherwise.   Am I good?
Yes, when beloved, I am goodness itself.   Am I
unselfish?   Oh, I can be *so* unselfish that I have
no thought except for somebody else. . . .'

Alice wishes to share the work to which
Charles has devoted his life, and she is in
despair when outward circumstances make him
withdraw from her.   It is her absolute claim to
sacrifice all to the one great important thing : to
remain true to one's self, one's vocation, one's
love.   All this is Sonia over again.

And when we see Alice in the second drama,
her violent rupture with the past, her sacrifice of
wealth and position, in order to live in a garret
with Charles, and to work with him,—it is Sonia,
as she dreamt she should have acted, had this
happy choice been left to her.

I have no doubt that her own pen, in describ-
ing these scenes, would have given them a much
warmer and more personal colour than I have
been able to give.

Alice's dream of a ' People's Palace ' on Herr-
hamra, of a great Workmen's Association, her

words: 'Think how differently things would have turned out, if we had all had the same education, the same mode of living; if we were all one great society of equals;' are they not Sonia Kovalevsky's own dreams, her own words?

A friend of hers told me, after her death, that once, when her husband had telegraphed to her that through a successful speculation he thought he had made a colossal fortune, she immediately laid the plan of founding a phalanstère.

A Danish author says, in speaking of 'Struggle for Happiness': 'I confess that I love this remarkable drama, which proves the omnipotence of love with mathematical stringency; that love, and love alone, is the essence of life, makes for strength and growth, and even enables us to do our duty.'

On reading these lines, I only regretted that they were spoken too late to give Sonia the joy it would have been to her to find herself so well understood.

The re-moulding of our work took much more time than the first writing. It was not finished, even, when we parted for the summer.

XI

DISAPPOINTMENTS AND CARES

WE had intended to spend this summer together. The new firm, Corvin-Leffler, meant to
go to Berlin and Paris, in order to seek literary
and dramatic acquaintances, which might be of
use later on, when our great work should be
ready to make its triumphant procession through
the world. However, all these illusions fell to
the ground one after another.

Our departure had been fixed for the middle
of May; we were looking forward to it with
intense joy, as if new fields of fame and interest
were about to open to us, when once more a dis-
tressing message from Russia crossed all our plans.
Sonia's sister was again in imminent danger;
her husband had to leave her in great haste to
go to Paris. There was no choice for Sonia but
once more to undertake the sad journey to this

bed of suffering, and to abandon all thought of pleasure and refreshment.

All her letters this summer show how depressed her spirits were.

'My sister continues in the same state as last winter; she suffers much, looks dreadfully miserable, and has no strength to move, and yet I do not think she is quite without hope of recovery. She is so glad that I have come, and keeps saying that she should certainly have died if I had refused to come to her now.

'I am so low to-day, that I will not write any more. The only thing enjoyable to think of is our fairy world and Væ Victis. . . .'

These words refer to two new plans for collaboration, which we had formed in the course of the spring.

In a later letter, she writes:

'I try to work again now, and in every free moment, I think of my mathematical problem, or I meditate on Poincaré's essays. I have not spirit enough for literary work—everything seems so dull and uninteresting. I prefer mathematics under these circumstances. It is pleasant to enter into a world quite outside one's self, and to speak of impersonal subjects. Only you, my dear, my unique Ann Charlotte, are always the

old dear one. I cannot say how I am longing
for you. We must remain friends to the end of
our lives. What would my life be without you?'

And in another letter :

' My brother-in-law has made up his mind to
remain in St Petersburg until my sister is able
to go to Paris with him. So I have made my
sacrifice quite in vain. If I knew that you were
free, I should now be able to meet you in Paris,
though, to tell the truth, the events here have
quite taken away my wish for amusement. I
should much prefer to settle down in some place
where I might work in peace, do no matter what,
mathematics or literature, if only it could make
me forget myself and everybody else. If you
are longing for me as much as I am for you, I
should be very happy to go wherever you are.
But if your summer is entirely taken up, which
I think most probable, I shall remain here for a
few weeks more, and then return to Stockholm,
where I shall settle down somewhere amongst
the rocks and work with all my might. I am not
now going to make arrangements for pleasure.
You know I am a fatalist, and I think I read in
the stars that I must not expect anything good
this summer ; so it is better to content one's self,
and make no vain efforts.'

From this summer dates a humorous letter, which I quote as characteristic of Sonia's satirical vein. She was never very careful with her letters or tidy with anything, so when I sent her confidential letters, I used to warn her very seriously not to leave them open on the table. Once she answered as follows :—

'Poor Ann Charlotte, the fear that your letters might fall into the wrong hands seems to have become a chronic disease with you. The symptoms of your illness get more and more alarming, and I am beginning to get very un- easy about you. I cannot help thinking that a person with such an illegible hand-writing as yours ought to feel at ease on this point. I assure you, except a few persons who have a direct interest in the matter, scarcely anybody would have patience to decipher your pot-hooks. As for your last letter, of course it went wrong the first time at the post-office. When I got it at last, with its blot on the envelope, I made haste to spread it on my table for the inspection of my servants and the whole G. family. They all found it particularly well written and most interesting. To-day I mean to pay a visit to Professor Mouton, as I wish to speak to him about translations from the Polish. I shall take

the letter with me and try to drop it in his reception room. That is all I can do to make your
name famous.'

When we met again in autumn, we undertook
the definite re-casting of our double drama; but
the joy, the enthusiasm, the illusions were gone
and this last correction was quite mechanical.
Already in November, the printing began, and
at the same time it was submitted to the man-
ager of the theatre. Proof-reading took up the
last part of the autumn. Towards Christmas
the work was published. The critics condemned it, and shortly after it was rejected by
the theatre.

Sonia did not take the thing very much to
heart. In fact, we had both become rather indifferent to the work. We quite sympathised
in loving only the unborn generations, and in
dreaming of other works of which we hoped
greater success. There was this difference, however, that Sonia kept clinging to the idea of
collaboration, whilst I had abandoned it long
ago, though I dared not tell her so. And, who
knows, perhaps it was this wish of reconquering
myself, of recovering my independence of
thought and feeling, which ripened my resolution to go to Italy that winter. This journey

had been planned long ago, but Sonia had continually opposed it as a treason to our friendship. The tie that bound me to her, which in many ways was precious to me and gave me so much joy, at the same time was becoming somewhat oppressive. Sonia's idealist nature claimed an entire merging into one another of two souls, which real life seldom offers, and which she could find neither in friendship nor in love.

Perhaps this explains to a certain extent, that even her maternal feeling could not satisfy her craving for tenderness. A child does not love as intensely as it is loved; it cannot quite take up the interests of somebody else, it is more passive than active in its feelings.

I don't mean to say that Sonia expected more than she gave; on the contrary, she bestowed the warmest sympathy, and overwhelmed her friends with tokens of affection. But she claimed a full share in return, and could not be satisfied unless she felt that she was as much to her friends as they were to her.

This same winter had brought her a deep and bitter grief. Her sister, to whose sick-bed she had hurried so often over land and sea, sacrificing all her own plans and wishes in order to be with her in her last moments, had been taken to

Paris to undergo an operation. Sonia at that time was bound by her university lectures, still, if she had been called she would have gone once more at the risk of losing her position and income. But she was assured that the operation was not dangerous, and that there was every reason to hope for full recovery. She had already been informed of the successful operation, when suddenly a telegram brought the news of her sister's death. Inflammation of the lungs had set in, and in her state of extreme weakness the patient had succumbed at once.

As we see from Sonia's early recollections, she had always loved this sister very fondly; so she felt the loss of her deeply, and grieved much at not having been with her in her last moments. Aniuta's fate had been bitter indeed. Once so bright and clever, admired by all, she became the victim of a long and painful disease. Besides, her life had been full of disappointments, she became unhappy in her personal relations, hampered in her career as an authoress—and at last, death, the inevitable, carried her away in the bloom of her age.

Sonia also felt very keenly, that with her sister's death the last link had snapped which bound her to the home of her childhood.

But she had a great amount of self-control, so
in society nobody saw her real feelings. She
did not even wear mourning—her sister, like
herself, had had an aversion to black, and she
thought it would have been mere conventionality
to mourn over her in that way. But in her
heart she fretted and pined, and became very
nervous and irritable in consequence. She kept
hoping that her sister would find some way of
revealing herself to her, either in a dream or in
a vision. For she retained throughout her life
that faith in dreams which is mentioned by her
early friend, as well as in forebodings and reve-
lations under other forms.

Indeed, she always knew beforehand whether a
year would be lucky or unlucky to her. Thus
she was positive that the year 1887 would bring
her a great joy and a great sorrow; that 1888
would be one of the happiest in her life, and
1890 one of the bitterest; 1891 would bring a
new dawn of light. This dawn was to be
death.

She used to have painful dreams when any of
those she loved suffered or did anything that
would make her suffer. The last few nights
before her sister's death her dreams had been
bad—to her own surprise, as the news were good.

But when the message came that she was dead, Sonia said she ought to have been prepared for it.

The revelation after death, which she had anticipated, did not occur.

XII

TRIUMPH AND DEFEAT. ALL
GAINED—ALL LOST

I LEFT in January 1888, and we did not meet
again till September 1889. So scarcely two
years had elapsed ; but each of us had passed
through the most important crisis of her life
during this interval, and we were both very
much changed. We could not approach one
another as in former days, each being absorbed
in the great drama of her own life, and neither
could tell the other the whole truth about the
conflict in which she was engaged.

As I have made it my particular task to
repeat what Sonia told me about herself, I shall
follow the same rule with regard to this last
great event of her life, though my statements
in this case are necessarily less accurate and

I

satisfactory, as she did not allow me now to look into her innermost heart, as she formerly used to do.

Shortly after my departure for Italy, she had made the acquaintance of a man, who, she said, was the most original and interesting character she had ever met. From the very first, he had inspired her with the strongest sympathy and admiration, and by degree, this feeling had developed into passionate love. He, on his side, had admired her, and paid her warm attention; he had even asked her to become his wife. But she felt as if he had been attracted, more from admiration than from love, and therefore, very naturally, she had refused to marry him; but now, it became her great object to conquer him entirely, to make his affection equal to her own. This struggle formed the whole history of her life during our separation. She tormented him and herself with her impossible claims, and her passionate jealousy; sometimes they would part in a fury—Sonia in deep despair; then they would meet and be reconciled, only to have the same scenes over again.

The letters to me from this period, reflect very little of her inner life. It was her nature to be very reserved in all that concerned her deepest feelings, particularly her griefs, and it was only under the influence of our personal intercourse, that she melted and became communicative. Consequently, it was not till I returned to Sweden, that I learned what I know about her history during my absence. Nevertheless, I shall quote extracts from the most characteristic parts of her correspondence of this period.

' Thanks for your letter from Dresden. I am always delighted to get a few lines from you, though this letter, on the whole, made a very melancholy impression. Well, what can we do? such is life, we don't get what we wish, and what we fancy we want ; everything else, but not that. Somebody else obtains the happiness I wanted, and of which perhaps he never thought. There must be something wrong with the waiting at life's great festival, as it seems that all the guests get portions which were meant for others.

' However, N. (Frithjof Nansen) seems to have got the portion he wanted ; he is in such raptures with his intended Greenland expedition that in his eyes no bride could equal it. . . . I am afraid nothing could induce him to give up travelling to the manes of the great dead, who, according to the Laplandic legend, are soaring over the icefields in Greenland.

'As for me, I am working hard at my competition-problem, though without particular enthusiasm.'

Sonia had recently made the acquaintance of Frithjof Nansen during his visit to Stockholm, and his personal appearance, as well as his daring schemes, had inspired her with profound interest. They had met only once, but the mutual impression had been so deep, that both afterwards thought this sympathy might have led to a decisive result between them, if circumstances had not kept them apart. In her next letter, from January 1888, she writes again : 'At present I am taken up entirely with the most deeply interesting article I have ever read. It was sent me to-day by Nansen, and contains the plan of his forthcoming expedition across the icefields of Greenland. It made me quite sad to read it. A Danish merchant has offered to contribute 5000 crowns towards the expenses, and I suppose no power on earth could keep Nansen back. The article is so full of interest, and so well written, that I shall send it to you as soon as I know your exact address (of course, you promise to return it immediately); this article will give you an approximate idea of the man. To-day I spoke to B. about him, and he says that Nansen's works are simply those of a genius, and that he is too good to be risking his life in Greenland.'

In Sonia's next letter we notice the first token of the crisis which was now to come. There is no date, but it must have been written in March the same year. She had now met the man whose influence was to become paramount for the last years of her life. She writes :—

'You put other questions to me ; but, as I cannot even answer them to myself, you must excuse my leaving them unanswered to you. I am afraid of making plans for the future. The only thing, alas, I can say for certain, is that now, for ten long endless weeks, I shall have to remain alone here in Stockholm. But, perhaps it is as well that I should see clearly how lonely I am indeed.'

I had repeated to her what Scandinavians in Rome had told me, that several years previously Nansen had engaged himself to be married to a German lady. To this I got the following reply :—

'DEAR ANN CHARLOTTE,—

'Souvent femme varie,
Bien folle est qui s'y fie!'

'If I had received your letter with the
dreadful news a few weeks ago, no doubt it
would have broken my heart, but now, to my
own shame, I must confess that on receiving
your warm and sympathising lines yesterday,
I burst out laughing. Yesterday, by the by,
was a bad day for me, for big M. left in the
evening. I hope some member of the family
has written to you about the change in our
plan, so that I need not enter upon this subject
to-day. I must say this change will be good
for me as well, for if M. had remained here,
I don't know how I should have worked. He is
so big, so grand (as K. justly remarked in his
speech), he occupies so much room, not only
on one's sofa, but also in one's thoughts, that
in his presence it would be quite impossible for me
to think of anything but him. Though we have
been constantly together during the ten days
he spent in Stockholm, generally by ourselves,
and talking of nothing but ourselves, with
marvellous sincerity, I am quite incapable of
analysing my feelings for him. The best

expression I can give of what he seems to me
are these excellent lines by Musset :—

> ' " Il est très joyeux—et pourtant très-maussade ;
>   Détestable voisin—excellent camérade ;
>   Extrêmement futile—et pourtant très-posé ;
>   Indignement naïf—et pourtant très-blasé ;
>   Horriblement sincère—et pourtant très-rusé." '

> (He is very cheerful—yet very gloomy ;
>   Detestable neighbour—yet excellent companion ;
>   Extremely frivolous—yet very serious ;
>   Dreadfully naïf—yet most fastidious ;
>   Shockingly sincere—yet very cunning.)

And a genuine Russian into the bargain.

'Certainly he has more original genius in his
little finger than you could squeeze out of many
others together, even if you used a hydraulic
press for the purpose. . . . So, from May 15th
till June 15th, I think I shall be in Paris, and
from thence we intend to go to Italy with M.,
and to meet you, for we have quite settled to
spend the summer there together. . . . M.'s
company always makes me wish to write novels,
for in spite of his huge dimensions (which by
the by are quite suitable to a Russian bojar),
he is the most perfect hero for a novel (of
course, a realistic one) whom I have ever met
in my life. And indeed, I also think he has
the right spirit for a good literary critic.'

Our plan to meet this summer came to nothing. Sonia joined her new Russian friend in London, at the end of May. Later on, she made a journey to the Hartz, in order to meet Weierstrass, and to get his advice with regard to the definite form of her work. In the spring she had sent an unfinished copy to the French Academy, requesting permission to present a more complete solution of the question later on, before the distribution of prizes took place. She worked excessively during this spring, and consequently I got but short letters. One from Stockholm is addressed to my brother and myself—we were together in Italy at the time :—

'My Dear Friends,—I cannot write long letters to you, for I work as much as it is possible for me or any human being to work. I do not know yet whether I shall be able to finish my treatise or not. There is a difficulty I cannot overcome, and I have written to Weierstrass to ask for his help. If he cannot help me, I am lost.'

In September, she came back to Stockholm, and throughout the autumn she lived in a state of over-excitement, which broke down her strength for a long time. This year—1888—as she had long foreseen, was to bring her to the zenith of honour and fortune, but at the same time, it contained the germs of the griefs and troubles which overwhelmed her the following year.

When at the solemn meeting of the French Academy of Science, on Christmas Eve 1888, in presence of a large assembly of the greatest contemporary men of science, Sonia appeared in person, and received the Prix Bordin, which was not only the greatest scientific distinction ever bestowed on a woman, but also one of the highest to which any man could aspire, that man was near her in whose society she had found the fullest satisfaction of all the cravings of her heart and mind. At this moment she possessed as much of the happiness of life as she had ever dreamt of: the most glorious acknowledgment of her genius, and an object of her ardent love. But she was like the princess in the fairy-tale, in whose cradle the fairies had put all good gifts; but a jealous fairy had added the one drawback, that these treasures should always be given her at the wrong time, or under circumstances that prevented her from fully enjoying them. While she was straining herself to the utmost to win the prize, which it had now become a point of honour for her to obtain, as all her friends among the mathematicians knew that she was competing for it, the new crisis in her personal life occurred, for which she had been yearning so long. She lived in a torturing conflict between the claims of womanhood and those of science; wearing out her physical strength, besides, by constant night work.

Sonia herself dimly felt, though it was not expressed in words, that the feelings of her friend began to cool when he saw her so entirely absorbed by her work, just at the moment when the bond between them seemed to be strongest. Very likely he looked upon this work as a gratification of vanity, and of a craving for honour and distinction—an honour, moreover, which does not help to render a woman attractive in a man's eye. The triumphs of a singer or of an actress often conquer a man's heart, also the beauty of a woman admired in society; but how can a man's fancy be captivated by a woman whose studies dim her eyes and wrinkle her brow, in order that she may win laurels on the field of science? These were Sonia's melancholy reflections.

She felt bitterly that it was foolish of her not
to sacrifice her vanity and ambition at this
moment, in order to gain that which she valued
more than all triumphs in the world; and yet—
she could not do it. To withdraw now would be
a striking acknowledgment of incapacity; the
power of circumstances, as well as her own
nature, pushed her irresistibly on towards the
goal which she had placed before her eyes. Had
she known beforehand the price she would have
to pay for putting off this work till the last
moment, she would scarcely have wasted her time
on that 'Struggle for Happiness,' which rendered
her present struggle for happiness so much
harder than it need have been.

Well, she came to Paris, and received her
prize. She was the heroine of the day. There
was a succession of fêtes, interviews, and visits;
all her time was taken up. Scarcely a moment
was left for the man who had come to Paris on
purpose to witness her triumph. And so it came
to pass that the fulfilment of her heart's desire, as
well as the gratification of her highest ambition,
coming simultaneously, were both spoilt, whereas
each, coming separately, would have filled her
with intense delight.

Her friend gave her the choice between him-

self and her scientific career. It was impossible
for her to make the sacrifice ; so the crisis came,
in which the happiness of her heart suffered its
great shipwreck.

A letter from this time, written to my brother,
shows how miserable she felt :—

'PARIS, *Jan.* 1889.

' DEAR GÖSTA,—I have this moment received
your kind letter. How grateful I am for your
friendship! I truly believe it is the only really
good thing life has brought me. I feel quite
ashamed to have done so little to show how
highly I value it! Forgive me, dear Gösta ;
really I have no control over my feelings at this
moment. Letters of congratulation are pouring
in from all sides, but, by a strange irony of fate,
I never felt so miserable as now. I am as miserable as a dog. No ; I hope, for their sake, that
dogs cannot be as unhappy as human creatures,
especially as women.

' Maybe I shall become more reasonable in
time, at least I shall make great efforts to get
over this state of mind. I shall take up work,
and try to interest myself in practical matters
again. Of course I shall be guided by your
advice. At present, all I can do is to keep my

grief to myself, take care not to commit myself
in society, and avoid becoming the subject of
gossip.   I have had many invitations this week
. . . . but I feel too wretched to-day to give
you an account of all these festivities. . . . When
I come home, I keep walking up and down in
my room.   I can neither eat nor sleep, and my
whole nervous system is in a deplorable state.   I
don't know if I should care for a temporary dispensation from official work. . . .

'Good-bye for the present, dearest Gösta.   Be
always my friend; I am deeply in need of it,
you may be sure.   Give my love to Foufi, and
thank S. for all the trouble she takes with her.—
Yours, with warm affection.

'S.'

She made up her mind to ask for a release
from work for the spring term, and remained in
Paris, whence she wrote to me :—

'Above all, let me congratulate you upon your
great happiness. . . . It has long been evident
to me that your destiny was happiness, mine
continual struggle.   Strangely enough, the
longer I live the more I feel inclined to believe
in fatalism, or rather, in determinism.   More

and more I lose faith in the free will man
is supposed to possess. I have an almost
physical sensation of my powerlessness to
change one iota of my fate, struggle as I may.
Now I am almost resigned; I work because
I cannot help it, but I have given up
hoping, even wishing, anything. You have
no idea to what a degree I have become
indifferent to everything. . . . But enough of
this; let us talk about other things. I am
delighted that you like my Polish story, and I
need not say how pleased I should be, if you
would translate it into Swedish. . . .

'I have also written a long tale about my
childhood and my sister, her first steps on the
literary career, and our connection with Dostojevsky. . . .'

In August she writes from Sèvres, where she
had settled with her daughter and a few Russian
friends :—

'I have just received a letter from your
brother, telling me that I shall probably meet
you on my return to Sweden. I confess that I
am selfish enough to feel delighted at this prospect. . . .

'I have never been in want of subjects for novels, but at this moment they are positively swarming in my head. . . . I wonder when I shall get time to finish all this.'

XIII

LITERARY WORK. TOGETHER
IN PARIS.

IN the middle of September Sonia returned to Stockholm, and we saw each other again after two years' separation. I found her very much altered. Her former cheerfulness was gone; the little furrow between her eye-brows had deepened; there was a gloom about her face; her eyes looked absent, and had lost their peculiar radiance, one of her chief attractions, and the little cast in them was more conspicuous than before. As usual, when among strangers she was able to hide the state of her mind, and to appear almost as she used to be; but to us, her intimate friends, the change was but too evident. She had quite lost her taste for society, even for that of her friends. She was too restless to be idle; only excessive work could give her a little peace.

She resumed her lectures from a sense of duty, but without interest. Literary work was now the conductor for her consuming restlessness, partly because she had not yet recovered sufficiently from her over-fatigues to enable her to take up science. What she wrote of 'Væ victis' dates from this time. It shows the melancholy strain of her mind; she meant to relate part of her own history in this novel. It was to be a tale of those who had suffered defeat in their struggle for happiness. Then she put the last touches to the 'recollections of her childhood.' In fact we both worked ardently for three months, though not together. It was like a feeble echo of former days—the days of our collaboration.

Neither Sonia nor I felt inclined to spend Christmas at home this year. We made up our minds to go on a journey together; this had often been planned, but we had never been able to carry it out. Our choice fell upon Paris, as the place where we should be most likely to form literary and stage connections, which we thought would be the best means of diverting our thoughts from personal griefs. So we started together in December. Neither of us, however, expected much pleasure from this

K

journey; it was only a kind of narcotic to calm our minds. There we were, saddening one another with our melancholy faces. We stopped a few days in Copenhagen, where Sonia's friends were struck by the change they noticed in her. Her face was worn and wrinkled, and she had a bad cough. She had caught cold during the influenza epidemic in Stockholm, and had never taken care of herself. One day, after having received a letter which excited her very much, she got out of her bed where she was lying with fever, put on a few clothes, went out into a snowstorm, came home dripping wet, and sat up late without changing her clothes.

When I besought her to take care of herself, she answered, 'Don't be afraid, I shan't get really ill, you may be sure. It would be too delightful to pass away now; I shan't have that luck.'

Sad indeed was our arrival in Paris, which in former days we used to picture to ourselves in the brightest colours. Paris, Sonia's favourite city, where she had always wished to live, was like a dead city to her now. The letters that had arrived gave us much to think of; Sonia's was not from him, but from one of his friends, and anything but satisfactory.

We spent some busy, turbulent weeks in this city, where the year before Sonia had been overwhelmed with honours and flattery, but where she seemed almost forgotten now. She had had her 'quart d'heure.'

We visited friends, made new acquaintances, and were on the move from morning till midnight. Yet I saw nothing of the place, no curiosities, not even the Eiffel Tower. We only hurried from one excitement to the other, and frequented the most heterogeneous circles—a most interesting mixture of types and nationalities: Russians, Jews, Poles, French, Scandinavians, people of the 'haute finance,' of science and of literature, exiles, conspirators, etc., etc. Sonia, of course, paid visits to mathematical celebrities, and received invitations from them, but she took less interest in these people now, as her mind was occupied with anything but mathematics. We spent one delightful day at the house of the Norwegian author Jonas Lie. Indeed, he was the only person who fully understood Sonia. We were invited to dinner to meet Grieg and his wife, who were just celebrating their great triumph in Paris. Lie made a speech in honour of Madame Kovalevsky, which touched her to tears. There was a peculiarly genial and festive atmosphere in our little circle; we all enjoyed each other's company, and felt that we were understood and appreciated

Jonas Lie was in excellent spirits. In his speech to Sonia he did not pay homage to the woman of science, nor to the authoress, but he spoke to 'little Tania Rajevski, who had won his heart, and with whom he felt deep sympathy. He was so sorry for the child, who was longing for affection, and whom nobody understood. Later on, life had showered all its gifts upon her—honour, distinction, and triumph; but there the child stood, still with her large wistful eyes, stretching out her empty hands. What did she want, this little girl? She only wanted a kind hand to give her an orange.'

'Thank you, Mr Lie,' Sonia exclaimed, with her sweet voice full of emotion, 'I have received many toasts in my life, but never one so charming!'

She could not say any more, but sat down and swallowed her tears with a glass of water. On going home that night she felt happier than she had done for a long while.

So, after all, there was one who understood her, though he knew nothing of her personal circumstances, who had only seen her twice or three times, but who, nevertheless, had learned from her book to look more deeply into her life than others, who had been her friends for many years. Then there might be some satisfaction in writing, something to live for after all.

We had to go to another party the same evening, but as Sonia was constantly expecting letters she could never stay away from the hôtel for many hours, so we dropped in and put the usual question to the porter, 'Any letters?' The next moment Sonia had grasped one and flew upstairs with it. I followed slowly and went to my own room, as I did not want to disturb her; but she rushed into my room, threw herself on my neck, burst into tears, and exclaimed, 'O God, I am *so* happy, *so* happy! I cannot bear it; I die, I am *so* happy!'

The letter cleared up an unfortunate mistake which had tortured her for the last few months to such a degree that she had become a shadow of herself. On the following night she left Paris, in order to meet the man on whom her whole fate now depended.

XIV

THE FLAME THREATENS TO EXPIRE

A FEW days after Sonia had left I received a line from her. The flame which had blazed up so high and filled her heart with exulting hopes was extinguished already. I have not kept her letter, but I remember its contents.

'I see that he and I will never fully understand one another. I shall return to Stockholm and work. Work must be my only consolation hereafter.'

And then all was over. No more letters from her this whole winter, nor the following spring, except a few affectionate lines in May, congratulating me on my wedding. She suffered, and she did not want to show her wound to me, who, she knew, was happy. She could never write on indifferent matters, so she kept silent. At the time this silence pained and hurt me very much; afterwards I understood that she could not have acted otherwise.

In April, the same year, 1890, she went to
Russia. She had hopes of being made an
ordinary Academician in St Petersburg, which
would have been the most profitable appointment she could ever wish to obtain, with a high
salary and no obligations except to spend two
months every year in St Petersburg. At the
same time it was the greatest scientific distinction which could be conferred in Russia. It
would have released her from her obligations in
Stockholm, and given her the chance of carrying
out her old wish : to make Paris her permanent
residence. She used to say to me while we were
there : 'If we cannot have the best thing life can
give, a happy love, at any rate life is bearable
if it offers us the next best thing, surroundings
which are congenial to our mind. But to have
neither is unbearable.'

I knew nothing of her plans till the beginning
of June, when we met quite unexpectedly in
Berlin, where my husband and I were staying
on our way to Sweden, and where Sonia had
arrived from St Petersburg the same day. This
time I found her in the gayest humour. People
who did not know her would have thought her
perfectly happy, but I knew better ; it was her
way of hiding the wounds of her heart. She had

been much admired in Helsingfors and St Petersburg, had hurried from feast to feast, met a number of highly distinguished persons, and made a speech in the presence of a thousand people. She assured me that she had enjoyed herself immensely, that she was very hopeful indeed; still there was something mysterious about her, and she would not speak out plainly. She anxiously avoided being alone with me as if afraid of being questioned. We spent a gay time together, talking and joking continually, but it was painful for me to notice how excited and restless she really was. She said nothing about her inner life, except that she meant never to marry.

She did not care to do like other women, who marry as soon as an opportunity offers, giving up their vocation and everything else. She had made up her mind to remain in Stockholm, either till she had got a better position somewhere else, or until she could make a sufficient income as an authoress.

However, she made no secret of having appointed to meet M. again, and to take a journey with him—her best friend and companion, as she called him.

Some months later we met again in Stock-

Sophie Kovalevsky.

1890.

holm, where she arrived in September for the new term. But her high spirits were gone, she was restless and depressed. I was not allowed to look into her heart, and she systematically avoided being alone with me. On the whole, she seemed rather indifferent to all who used to be her intimate friends. Evidently her soul was elsewhere, and she looked upon these months in Stockholm as a kind of exile, eagerly anticipating the Christmas vacations, when she would be able to go away again. The fact was, she could neither live with M. nor without him; it was a hopeless struggle indeed. She was like a plant which is taken out of its proper soil, yet cannot thrive in any other, and so is bound to die.

My brother, who had moved to Djursholm, outside Stockholm, wanted Sonia to come and live in his neighourhood, but though she was very sorry that he had left town, she could not make up her mind to follow his example. 'Who knows how long I shall remain here?' she said, 'things cannot go on as they are now,' was her constant remark, 'and if I should happen to be in Stockholm again next winter, I should be so melancholy that you would not care to have me near you.'

This intolerable state of mind made her break

off all her connections; she neglected her friends, retired from society, dressed more and more carelessly, and became indifferent to her home. Her conversation lost most of its sympathetic charm and sparkling life. Her usual interest in all subjects of human thought and human life was almost gone; she was entirely absorbed in the tragedy of her own life.

XV

CONCLUSION

I SAW Sonia for the last time in this life on one
of the early days of December 1890. She had
come to Djursholm to take leave of us before
starting for Nice. None of us had the slightest
foreboding that this would be our last good-bye.
We had agreed to meet in Genoa immediately
after Christmas. But this was not to be. A
telegram was to have reached us on our return
to Italy, but, owing to a mistake in the address,
we did not receive it, and so, while Sonia and her
companion were waiting for us in Genoa, we
passed through the town without knowing that
she was there. On New Year's Day, which we
had hoped to spend together, she and her friend
visited the fine 'marble garden of the dead'
in Genoa. While there, a shadow suddenly
spread over Sonia's face, and she said these
words of sad foreboding : 'One of us will die

before the end of this year ; we have spent New
Year's day in a churchyard.'

Some weeks later, she was again on her way
to Stockholm. This journey, which she had
always detested, was this time not only to be the
most painful she had ever made, but also the
most fatal. Her heart bleeding with the bitter
pain of parting, feeling that these constant
separations would kill her, she sat in the railway
carriage shivering with cold. What a contrast
between the mild, fragrant atmosphere she had
left and the biting frost of the northern winter !
She detested cold and darkness as intensely as
she loved warmth and sunshine. And then,
instead of taking the most comfortable and
direct route to Stockholm from Berlin, where
she had spent some days, she chose a very
round-about way. She had heard that there
was an epidemic of smallpox in Copenhagen,
and, having a horror of this disease, she did not
want to run the risk of spending a night there.
So she chose the long, troublesome route across
the Danish islands. The constant changes on
this line, as well as the bad weather, probably
gave her the severe cold she caught on this
journey. In Fredericia, where she arrived late
at night, she could not take a porter for want of

Danish small coin, so she had to carry a good
deal of luggage herself, and over-fatigued as she
was, shivering with cold, and deeply depressed
in mind, no wonder that she felt as if she would
collapse. On her arrival in Stockholm, the 4th
February in the morning, she felt ill. Still she
worked all the next day, and delivered her
lecture on Friday, the 6th. She never missed
a lecture when she could help it. She even went
to a party at the Observatory the same evening.
But there an attack of fever came on; she
retired, but could not get a cab, and, helpless as
she was, never knowing her way in Stockholm,
she got into a wrong tram-car. It took her a
long time to get home by a round-about way,
and then she sat up the whole night, shivering
with fever, sad to death, feeling herself a prey to
the violent illness that had seized her. That
same day she had said to my brother, who was
the head of the University, that no matter at
what cost, she meant to get leave from her
work in April, in order to go abroad again. It
was her only comfort, when she came home in
despair, to lay plans for new journeys. In the
mean time, she meant to calm her restless mind
with work. She had several new schemes in her
eadh, and talked about them with great interest.

To my brother she explained the idea of a new mathematical work, which he thought would have become the most important of her productions. Amongst several novels which she intended to write, was one which she had already commenced, and in which she intended to give a character-study of her father. Another was to have the title, 'A Nihilist,' and to contain part of the history of Tschernyschevsky's life.

Often as Sonia had longed for death, she did not want to die just now. In fact, according to the friends who were living with her at the last, she was nearer resignation than she had ever been. She had ceased to hope for that perfect happiness, the ideal of which had been constantly, haunting her, but she still longed for the stray sunbeams of it which might fall upon her path.

And, in her innermost heart, she was afraid of the great unknown. She had often said, that only her uncertainty as to whether the future world brings punishment or not had prevented her from putting an end to her present life. She had no definite religious creed, but she believed in eternal life for the individual, and she trembled at the thought of it. Above all, she dreaded the moment when earthly life would cease, and often quoted Hamlet's words:

‘ For in that sleep of death what dreams may come,
When we nave shuffled off this mortal coil,
 , . Must give us pause. . . .’

And in her lively imagination, she pictured to
herself the awful moment when, perhaps, the
nervous system is still alive and suffering, while
the body is physiologically dead—indescribable
sufferings, perhaps, known only by him who has
made the plunge into the great darkness. She
approved very much of cremation, partly because
she was afraid of being buried alive, fancying
how dreadful it would be to awake in the coffin ;
and she described the situation so graphically
that it made one shudder. However, her illness
was so short and violent, that, at the last, I do
not think she had any sense of these things.
The only words which seemed to indicate that
she was aware of the approaching end were
spoken on Monday morning, the 9th, scarcely
twenty hours before her death : ‘ I shall never
recover from this illness ’; and in the evening :
‘ I feel as if a change had taken place within
me.’

She was unable to speak much, for she had
violent pains, high fever, and difficulty in breathing ; she was in an agony of fear, and could not
bear being left alone. The last night she said to

a friend, who scarcely ever left her bedside:
'When you hear me moan in my sleep, do call
me, and help me to change my position, or else
I am afraid I shall be very bad. My mother
died in such a fit of agony.' She suffered from
hereditary heart disease, which used to make her
say that she would die young. However, the
post-mortem examination showed that her heart
was not much affected, although the complaint
might have added to the asthma, caused by
pleurisy.

The friends who were with her during her
illness, spoke in the highest terms of her patience
and gentleness; she was afraid of giving the
least trouble, and grateful for every little service.
Her daughter being invited to a children's party,
she was anxious that she should not lose this
pleasure, and asked her friends to help in getting
what was wanted for the occasion. When the
little girl presented herself in the sickroom in
the gipsy costume she was to wear, an affectionate smile greeted her, and her mother wished
her much pleasure.

A few hours later the poor child was called
out of her sleep, and came just in time to receive
her mother's last dying glance, which rested on
her with fond love.

As the doctors had not thought there was any immediate danger, and rather fancied that the illness would be a lingering one, her friends had thought it would be better to spare their strength a little after several days' constant strain, and so they had gone to take some rest, leaving the patient in charge of an Elisabeth Sister.

And thus, this very night, the fatal hour struck! Sonia was sound asleep when her friends left her, but about two o'clock she awoke to the last dreadful struggle. Her agony began ; she showed no signs of consciousness, could neither move, nor talk, nor swallow. This lasted for two hours. Just at the last moment one of the two friends arrived whom the nurse had sent for too late.

Alone,—alone with a strange nurse, who could not even speak her language, she had to pass through this last bitter strife. Who knows what comfort a loved voice, a pressure of the hand, might have been to her during these awful two hours? I should have wished that a priest had read the Russian Mass to her. With her veneration for the Greek Church, as for all her early recollections, those well-known tones might have been soothing to her, if she could have heard them. Perhaps her trembling hands would have clasped the cross, which has comforted so many hearts in the hour of death, and which she had always loved as a symbol of human suffering. But nothing! nothing! No word of comfort, no help, no loving hand on the feverish brow—alone in a foreign country, with a tortured heart, hopeless, perhaps trembling for the unknown—such was her end on earth—this 'soul of fire and soul of thought.'

.   .   .   .   .

Out of the hopeless gloom which, during my first grief, seemed to surround this death-bed now and then a ray of light would emerge.

Whether life be long or short does not signify so much, all depends upon its fruitfulness to ourselves and to others. And seen from this point of view, Sonia's life was longer than most people's; she had lived intensely, drunk deep draughts of the wells of joy and grief, and of the treasures of science, had reached heights to which only imagination can lift one; and she had made others share in the treasures of her heart, her experience and her fancy. Hers was the kindling voice which belongs to genius, if it does not isolate itself in egotism. Nobody who lived with her, for ever so short a time, could remain uninfluenced by this wonderfully bright intelligence and warm feeling ; it fertilised every germ of life that came within her sphere.

Her highest aim was fellowship, spiritual fellowship, and though she may have been too fantastic in her superstitious dreams and forebodings, certainly she had something in her of the prophetic vision. When she looked straight into your face, turning her short-sighted sparkling eyes on your own, you felt that she pierced your soul through and through. Many a time one glance of hers would be sufficient to penetrate the mask with which some people succeed in hiding their real face from unsuspicious eyes, and many a time she detected secret motives which were hidden to all others, even to the person in question. Her poetic gift, too, was prophetic ; a word, an insignificant event, might reveal a whole life's history to her.

It was her great object to find the logical connection between all manifestations of life, as for instance, between the laws of thought and the outward phenomena. She could not satisfy herself with seeing in part, and understanding in part ; it was her delight to dream of a more perfect form of life, where, according to the apostle, 'we shall see no longer in part, but face to face.' To see the unity in the variety was the aim and end of all her philosophy and her poetry.

Has she reached this end now? Our thought cannot fathom this possibility, but our heart beats with a trembling hope which breaks the point of death's bitterness.

Besides, she had always wished to die young. Though hers seemed an inexhaustible well of life, ready for every new impression, open to every joy, great or small, in the innermost recess of her heart there was a thirst, which this life could never satisfy. As her mind craved absolute truth, absolute light, so her heart craved absolute love—a completeness which human life does not yield, and which her own character in particular rendered impossible. It was this discord that consumed her. If we start from her own belief in a fundamental connection between all phenomena of life, we see that she was bound to die, not because some strong and destructive microbes had settled in her lungs, or because the chances of her life had not brought her the happiness she desired, but because the necessary organic connection between her inward and outward life was missing; because there was no harmony between her thought and her feeling,

her temperament and her character. If there is
a world where these contrasts can be reconciled,
she is happy now; if not, she has reached
harmony, in so far as in complete rest there is
harmony.

We seldom see a death call forth so great
and general sympathy as hers. From nearly all
parts of the civilised world telegrams of con-
dolence poured in. From the highly con-
servative St Petersburg Academy, of which for
the last year she had been a corresponding
member, from the Sunday School children in
Tiflis, from the Teachers' Society in Charchow
—general homage was paid to her memory.
Russian women resolved to erect a monument
on her tomb in Stockholm; cartloads of flowers
covered the black spot surrounded by white
snowheaps in the churchyard.

But out of all these honours and incense her
image rises as on a pedestal, impersonal and inaccessible. To posterity she appears exactly
what she did not want to be, a kind of mental
giant with unusually developed and finely
constructed brain, so far above the ordinary
proportions, that she is looked upon with more
admiration than sympathy.

Through my detailed and unveiled image of

her life, with its shortcomings and humiliations, as well as with its greatness and its triumphs, I may have reduced these dimmensions to more ordinary proportions. But keeping in view the task I had undertaken, to try to represent her as I knew she wished to be seen and understood, I have considered it very important to point out the ordinary human features in her portrait, which brought her nearer to the level of other women, making her their equal, not an exception—thus confirming the rule that the heart is the essential part, not only in a woman's, but in human nature, and that the ablest and the least gifted can meet in this focus of all human life.

LIFE IN RUSSIA

THE SISTERS RAJEVSKI

BY

SONIA KOVALEVSKY

I

EARLIEST CHILDHOOD

TANIA RAJEVSKI'S first recollections were all in one way or another connected with travels or travelling adventures. When in later years she would sit with her eyes closed, and recall to her memory the first conscious impressions of her life, she would see a broad dusty road lined with birch trees and milestones on each side, and a huge travelling carriage large enough for a Noah's ark, moving slowly along on the road. Now and then the dulness of the journey would be relieved, by attempts to throw Aniuta's doll out of the window, or by picking up stones. The nights were often spent at post-stations, in improvised beds made on hard narrow sofas, or simply on chairs. Tania's father, Ivan Sergejevitsch Rajevski, was a general in the artillery, and had to travel about a good deal

on official business. On these occasions he was
generally accompanied by his family.

When Tania was five years old, the Rajevskis
resided for some time in Kaluga. There were
three children, two daughters and a son. By
this time, Aniuta, the elder sister, was twelve
years old, Fedia, the brother, three. Their
nursery was a large low room, so low, that
Njania (Russian, nurse), touched the ceiling
when she stood on a chair. All three children
slept there. Aniuta was to have shared the
room of her governess—the French scarecrow,
as they called her—but she did not want to,
and so she remained with the others.

Njania had an enormous bed, which was her
pride: it was like a mountain of pillows and
eider-downs. Now and then the children were
allowed to climb up on the top of it, and it
was their great delight to plunge down into
this feathery deep.

There was always a peculiar smell in this
nursery—a mixture of incense, tallow candle,
oil, and birch-balm, which Njania used for her
gout.

The governess never entered this room without
holding her pocket-handkerchief to her nose, to
keep out the disgusting smell.

'You really must open the window, Njania!'
she exclaimed in her bad Russian.

Njania takes this order as a personal injury.

'The idea!' she grumbled between her teeth.
'Foreign heathen! Why should I open the
window? The children might catch cold.'

Every morning there were skirmishes between
Njania and the governess.

It is late; sunshine fills the room; by and by
the children open their sleepy eyes, but they
don't think of getting up yet. The first thing
is to have a game in bed, pulling each other's
legs, chattering and fighting with pillows.

Then a pleasant smell of coffee fills the
room. Njania, who is only half-dressed, and
has exchanged her night-cap for a silk handkerchief—her invariable headgear during the
day, carries in a tray with a large copper can,
and gives the children their coffee and hot buns
in bed, unwashed and uncombed as they are.
After this, they often go to sleep again, tired
with the preceding game.

Suddenly the door opens with a rush, and on
the threshold appears the angry governess.

'Comment, vous êtes encore au lit, Annette?
il est onze heures; vous êtes de nouveau en
retard pour votre leçon!' she bursts out im-

patiently. 'How *can* you allow them to sleep so long? I shall tell the general,' she says, turning to Njania.

'Do, please, you old toady,' Njania mutters between her teeth, when the governess is out of the door. 'The general's own children! why shouldn't they be allowed to sleep as long as they like? Too late for lessons! well, what does it matter? You just wait a little, that won't hurt you.' However, in spite of her grumbling, Njania thinks she had better make a little haste; and indeed, if the preparations were long, the dressing does not take much time. Njania just hurries with a wet sponge over their faces and hands, draws a comb through their tangled hair, throws on their clothes—tidy or untidy, as the case may be,—and they are supposed to be ready.

Aniuta goes to her lessons, the other two remain in the nursery. Without minding their presence, Njania sweeps the floor, making clouds of dust fly, puts the quilts on the beds, shakes her own eider-downs, and the cleaning process is over. Tania and Fedia go to play on the sofa. They are seldom taken out for a walk, except in unusually fine weather, and on great festivals, when Njania goes to church with them.

As soon as lessons are over, Aniuta hurries
to the nursery, which she likes much better than
the schoolroom, especially as Njania receives
many visitors, who are fond of chatting, and
taking coffee with her.

The nursery door opens, and a beautiful young
lady appears in an elegant silk dress, with
flowers in her hair, and fine ornaments of gold
and jewels : it is Elena Paulovna, Tania's mother.
She is going to a party, and comes to say
good-bye to her children.

Aniuta runs to meet her, and covers her hands
and neck with kisses, then she examines her
ornaments. 'When I am a grown up lady I
shall be as beautiful as mamma,' she says, putting
on her mother's necklace, while she stands on
tiptoe, and admires herself in the looking-glass.

When Tania attempts to caress her mother,
or climbs on her lap, she always manages to do
some mischief, tearing her mother's dress, or
hurting her in some way or other ; then she gets
frightened, and hides herself in a corner. This
makes her a little afraid of her mother. Besides,
Njania often says that Aniuta and Fedia are
Elena Paulovna's pets, and that Tania is the
Cinderella in the family.

Aniuta being so much older than the others,

enjoyed great privileges; in fact, she had her
own way in everything. She went to the
drawing-room whenever she liked, and from
her earliest childhood, was admired for her
beauty and charming manners, as well as for
her clever answers. Tania and Fedia were only
allowed to appear on festive occasions; as a
rule, they lunched and dined in the nursery.

Now and then, Nastasja, Madame Rajevski's
maid, would rush into the nursery.

'Good Njania, be quick, put the light blue
silk frock on Fedia, her ladyship wants to shew
him to the guests.'

'And what about Tania?' Njania asks in a
tone as if she knew what the answer would
be.

'Tania isn't wanted, she had better stay here,
the dirty little thing,' and the maid laughs, well
knowing that Njania will be annoyed. And, indeed, she feels quite cross, and keeps walking up
and down in the room, muttering between her
teeth, while she throws pitying glances at the
little girl, and now and then strokes her hair:
'Poor thing! my poor little pet!'

It is night: Njania has put Tania and Fedia
to bed, but she has not taken off her silk handkerchief yet, this act which marks that work is

ended and rest begins. She is sitting on the
sofa with Nastasja.

The room is half dark ; only the dim flame of
a tallow candle, which Njania has forgotten to
snuff, and at the opposite end of the room the
flickering bluish light of a lamp that burns
before the image of a saint, are reflected from
the ceiling, where they form all kinds of
fantastic figures, and set off very distinctly
our Saviour's hand, which comes out from
beneath his silk mantle, and is held forth to
give the blessing.

Tania hears her brother's regular breathing,
and the heavy snoring of the job-girl, Fekluscha,
with the pug-nose, who lies on the floor before
the chimney, sleeping on a grey rug, which is
spread out there at night and stowed away in a
closet during the day.

Njania and Nastasja are whispering together ;
thinking the children are sound asleep, they gossip freely about domestic affairs. But Tania, who
does not sleep, listens attentively to their talk.
Much of it she does not understand, or does not
care for ; sometimes she goes to sleep without
hearing the end of it. However, the scraps
which she understands impress themselves deeply
on her mind and grow to fantastic dimensions in

her imagination, leaving indelible traces for her whole life.

'How can I help loving her best, the little mite?' Njania says, and Tania knows whom she means. 'Nobody but myself has ever nursed her. It was very different with the others. When Aniuta was born, her parents, grandparents and aunts never tired of admiring her—of course, she was the first. I never had her to myself for a moment; but it was very different with Tania.'

At this point in the oft-repeated tale, Njania used to lower her voice mysteriously, and of course Tania strained her ears to the utmost.

'The fact was, the poor creature arrived at the wrong moment,' Njania said in a whisper, 'The general had lost much money at cards in the English Club—her ladyship's jewels had to be pawned; how then could they rejoice that the Lord had given them a daughter, especially as both wanted a son? Her ladyship used to say to me, "You will see, Njania, I shall get a son this time!" And she prepared everything for a boy—crucifix, and bonnet with blue bows; so when it was a girl, after all, she grieved very much. But then, at last, when Fedia came, it was all right.'

Owing to this and similar stories, Tania very

soon convinced herself that she was only tolerated in her home, and this had a great influence
on her character. She became shy and reticent.
So, when taken to the drawing-room, she would
cling with both hands to Njania's dress, and look
very sullen. It was impossible to squeeze a
word out of her, Njania might try ever so hard.
She kept casting shy glances at the persons present, just like a hunted deer. At last her mother
would get impatient, and say to Njania, 'Take
her away, I am quite ashamed of her!'

She was also shy with other children, and
seldom had an opportuniny of seeing any.
When they were out walking she would sometimes see school-children romping about, and
ask Njania to allow her to play with them.
'What are you thinking of?' the nurse replied;
'You are a lady, you can't play with those common brats!' And this was said with such contempt and reproach that Tania felt quite ashamed
of herself. At last she lost all thought or wish
of playing with other children. When a little
girl of her own age happened to come on a visit,
Tania never knew what to say; she only kept
thinking, 'I wish she would go.'

Her whole happiness was to be alone with
Njania. In the evening, when Fedia was in bed,

and Aniuta had gone to the drawing-room, she crept up to nurse on the sofa, and Njania began telling her fairy tales. The child was deeply impressed, and would dream of the monsters she had heard of, the were-wolf, the twelve-headed serpent, etc.

In fact, she was on the way to grow up a sickly over-sensitive girl. But a new life was soon to begin for her.

II

PALIBINO. DOMESTIC DRAMAS

WHEN Tania was six years old, her father retired from the service, and the family went to live on his country estate Palibino, in the government of Vitebsk. At this time it was generally rumoured that serfdom was to be abolished, and this caused Ivan Sergejevitsch to pay more attention to the management of his property, which had hitherto been left in the hands of a steward. On the whole a great change was to take place with the Rajevskis. Carelessness and gaiety gave way to a more serious life.

Up till now Ivan Sergejevitsch had paid but slight attention to his children and their education, as he thought that these were matters for the wife, not for the husband. He had taken most notice of Aniuta, as the eldest; besides, she was clever. and he liked to show her off. When he heard complaints about her wilfulness and wild spirits, he might occasionally think right to put on a severe face, but she knew quite well that in his heart he was amused at her pranks and laughed at them. The little ones did not see much of their father; when he met them, he would just say a kind word and pinch their cheeks, that was all. Only on solemn occasions, when he was to go to some official parade and was dressed in his splendid uniform, the children were called to the drawing-room to see 'how fine their father was,' and this was a great treat to them; they would jump about and clap their hands in delight.

But shortly after they had moved to Palibino, an event occurred which drew attention to the nursery in a very unpleasant way, and made a profound impression on everybody, not least on Tania.

Objects began to disappear from the nursery, now one thing, now another. At first nobody made much fuss about it, but when by and by more expensive objects vanished, such as a silver spoon, a gold thimble, a knife, etc., there was a general stir and anxiety. Evidently there must be a thief in the house. Njania, who thought she was responsible for the children's property,

made up her mind to find the thief, cost what it
might.

Of course, the first suspicion fell on poor
Fekluscha, the nursery-girl. Certainly she had
served in the nursery for three years and nothing
of this kind had ever been noticed ; but according to Njania, this did not prove anything; she
had been too young to know the value of the
objects, ' but now she is older and knows better,'
Njania would say. ' She has relations down
there in the village, to whom of course she carries
the stolen goods,' and she would treat Fekluscha
so severely, that the poor girl, feeling instinctively that she was suspected, looked as if she
might really be guilty.

Closely as she observed the supposed culprit,
however, Njania could never catch her in the
very act. At the same time fresh objects disappeared, and the old ones never came back.
One day Aniuta's money-box was missing, which
had its place in Njania's cupboard, and contained
about forty rubles, if not more. The news of this
theft at last reached the general's ears. Njania
was called to her master, who gave her the per-
emptory order to find the thief immediately.
Now it was clear to all that the affair had become serious. Njania was in despair. Then it

happened one night that she awoke, hearing a
peculiar smacking sound from the corner where
Fekluscha was sleeping.   A suspicion flashed
upon her; she stretched out her hand carefully,
struck a match and lighted her candle.   And
what did she see?   There was Fekluscha crouch-
ing on the rug, with a large jam-pot between her
knees, gobbling the jam as fast as she could with
a crust of bread.

It must be noticed that a few days previously
the housekeeper had complained that a pot of
jam had disappeared from her cupboard.

To rush out of her bed and seize the girl's
hair was the affair of seconds.

'Have I caught you at last, you wretched
thief!   Where have you got that jam?   Can't
you tell!'   She seized the child and shook her
violently.

'Oh no, Njania dear! indeed I haven't taken
it, I assure you!' Fekluscha screamed.   'Maria
Vasiljevna gave me the pot last night, but she
said I wasn't to let you see it.'

But Njania had her great doubts as to this
statement.   'I don't think you are clever at
lying,' she said contemptuously, 'why should
Maria Vasiljevna think of giving you jam?'

'Oh dear, dear Njania, it isn't a lie!   I swear

it is the truth ; ask her yourself. I put her iron
to the fire yesterday, and then she gave me the
jam. She only said : ' Don't show Njania, she
will scold me for spoiling you.'

' All right, we shall see to-morrow morning,'
Njania answered ; and in the mean time she
shut up Fekluscha in a dark closet, where the
poor thing continued crying for a long while.

The next morning the inquiries began.

Maria Vasiljevna was a needlewoman, who
for many years had been living with the Rajevski
family. She was no bondwoman, and was
treated with much more consideration than the
other servants. She had her own room, where
she took her meals by herself, and was served
from the family table. As a rule, she was very
proud, and did not mix with the other servants.
The family valued her highly, because she was
very clever at her work ; ' she has fairy-fingers,'
they used to say. She might be about forty.
Her face was thin and worn, her eyes unnaturally
large and black. She was not good-looking, but
there was something distinguished about her, and
nobody would have taken her for an ordinary
needlewoman. She was neat and tidy in her
dress, and used to keep her room comfortable,
even with a certain elegance ; there were flowers

in the window, pictures on the walls, and a corner-bracket with all kinds of nick-nacks.

Besides, a peculiar interest was attached to Maria Vasiljevna, because of a romantic episode in her earlier life. She had been a healthy, fine young girl, staying as bondswoman with a lady who possessed an estate in the country, and who had a grown-up son. This young man was an officer. Once, during a visit to his mother, he had given Maria Vasiljevna some silver coins. Unfortunately the old lady had entered the servants' hall immediately after, and had seen the money in the girl's hand.

'Where did you get that money?' she asked severely, and Maria was so frightened that, instead of answering, she put the coins into her mouth, and swallowed them. A violent attack of illness was the consequence, and she fell down screaming with pain. They only just saved her life, but she was ill for a long time, and her beauty was gone for ever. The old lady died shortly afterwards, and her young master gave Maria her freedom.

Maria Vasiljevna used to pay frequent visits to the nursery, and the children liked to go to her room, especially at dusk, when she could not see to work, and would sit at the window with

her head on her hand, singing old sentimental
ballads in her melancholy voice: ' Through the
dark dales,' or ' Black flower, dark flower.' It
was sad, but for Tania these times had a peculiar
charm. Now and then Maria's singing would
be interrupted by a violent cough, which shook
her whole frame as if she was going to burst.
She had suffered from this cough for years.

When, on the morning after the scene with
Fekluscha, Njania asked Maria Vasiljevna if she
had given Fekluscha the jam, she looked utterly
astonished, as might be expected.

' Oh dear, Njania, what are you thinking of?
You don't think I would do such a thing, and
spoil the child like that? Besides, I have got
no jam myself,' she exclaimed in an offended
tone.

So, of course, the matter was clear; but
Fekluscha's impudence was so great that, in spite
of this, she persisted in declaring that she was
innocent.

' But, Maria Vasiljevna, for Christ's sake, have
you quite forgotten? You called me into your
room last night, then you thanked me for the
irons, and gave me the jam,' she cried in despair,
trembling all over, as if in fever.

' You are raving, Fekluscha, you must be ill,'

Maria Vasiljevna replied calmly, and her pale face did not betray the slightest emotion.

There was no further doubt as to Fekluscha's guilt. She was taken away, and shut up in a closet far away from the family apartments.

'There you may stay, you bad girl, and you won't get anything to eat till you confess,' Njania said, turning the key twice in the lock.

As a matter of course, this event created a great sensation all over the house. The servants, one by one, paid visits to Njania, and talked it over with her. The nursery had become a club-room.

Fekluscha's father was dead, but her mother lived in a neighbouring village, and was occasionally sent for to help in the laundry. Of course she soon heard what had happened, and rushed up to the nursery, crying and wailing, and protesting that her daughter was innocent. However, Njania soon silenced her.

'Hush, hush, be quiet, don't make such a fuss! You wait till we find out where your daughter has hidden the stolen things,' she said, and looked so severe that the poor woman was frightened, and retired in a hurry.

Public opinion was decidedly against Fekluscha. 'If she has taken the jam,' they said,

'she must have stolen the other things as well!'
And they were the more angry with her, as these
mysterious thefts, which had been going on for
weeks, had weighed on them all alike, a heavy
burden—each being afraid that he or she might
be suspected. So this discovery was a general
relief.

However, Fekluscha could not be induced to
confess. Njania visited her several times in the
course of the day. She kept repeating, ' I have
stolen nothing, may God punish Maria Vasiljevna for being so bad to me!' In the evening,
Elena Paulovna came to the nursery.

' Are you not too hard upon that poor girl?'
she said to Njania; 'it won't do to leave her
without anything to eat the whole day,' she
added in a despondent voice.

But Njania would not hear of mercy.

' What is your ladyship thinking of? Why
should we pity that creature? She has allowed
honest people to be suspected all the time, and
then it is she who is the thief after all!' she
answered in such a determined way, that Elena
Paulovna was silenced, and left the room without
obtaining any alleviation in the poor culprit's
fate. The following day Fekluscha persevered
in her denial, and her judge began to get a little

uneasy; but at noon Njania came running to her mistress, crying out triumphantly: 'She has confessed at last!'

'Well, and where are the things?' was Elena Paulovna's first question.

'That she hasn't told yet,' Njania answered with a little hesitation, 'she talks all kinds of rubbish and says she has forgotten, but she'll soon remember if she has to stay some hours longer where she is!'

And indeed, in the evening, Fekluscha made a complete confession, and gave a detailed account of the whole affair. She had stolen the things in order to sell them later on; but as she could not find an opportunity of doing so, she had hidden them under a rug in a corner of her room. At last, when the articles were missed, and search was made to find out the thief, she had been afraid, and wanted to put them back in their places, but she could not manage, so at last she had tied them up in a handkerchief and thrown them into a deep pond.

All had been so anxious to see the end of this painful business, that nobody thought of criticising Fekluscha's report. The family was vexed that the stolen goods had been destroyed, but nobody thought of doubting the fact.

The criminal was taken out of her prison, and the following just sentence was pronounced : she was to have a good whipping, and to be sent home to her mother.

In spite of Fekluscha's and her mother's lamentations and remonstrances, the sentence was carried out immediately, and another girl was engaged for the nursery.

After some weeks order seemed to be restored, and the whole event almost forgotten.

But one evening when everybody was at rest, and Njania was just going to bed, the nursery door was slowly opened, and in came Alexandra, the laundress, Fekluscha's mother. She had persistently denied her daughter's guilt, and had had several skirmishes with Njania about the matter, until at length the nurse had forbidden her to put her nose inside the nursery.

But this time there was such a peculiarly mysterious expression in her face, and Njania saw at once that she had something important on her mind.

'Look here, Njania,' she whispered, looking round anxiously lest somebody should hear her, and from beneath her apron she took out the little mother-of-pearl penknife, which used to be the children's delight, and which had been

among the stolen things, and was supposed to
have been thrown into the pond.

At this sight Njania folded her hands in
amazement. 'Wherever did you find that knife?'
she asked. 'Yes—where did I find it?' Alexandra answered slowly, then pausing some
moments and enjoying Njania's surprise. 'Phillip
Matvjejitsch, the gardener, gave me some old
trousers to mend, and in one of the pockets I
found this knife,' she exclaimed in a solemn
voice.

Phillip Matvjejitsch was a German by birth
and belonged to the upper servants; he was
unmarried, and had a very good salary. To an
impartial eye he was an elderly, fat, rather
unpleasant fellow with reddish whiskers, but
among the female servants he was considered
good-looking.

Njania was dumfounded and did not know
what to say.

'But how is it possible?' she exclaimed.
'Phillip Matvjejitsch never sets foot in the
nursery. How could he have got that knife?
Besides, a man like that wouldn't think of
stealing the children's things!'

Alexandra kept silent for some moments
looking at Njania with a long scornful glance;

then she put her mouth to her ear and whispered some words, in which the name of Maria Vasiljevna was often repeated.

At last a gleam of the truth flashed through Njania's bewildered brains.

'Oh, that's what it is!' she exclaimed. 'What a hypocrite, what a wicked creature! but wait a little, we shall soon let everybody see what you are!' She was in a fury.

Later on it appeared that Alexandra had suspected Maria Vasiljevna long ago; she had noticed her flirtation with the gardener. 'It isn't likely,' she said to Njania, 'that such a fine fellow should make love to such an old maid without getting something for his trouble! Of course, she has bribed him with presents.'

And indeed, she soon found out that Maria Vasiljevna gave him money as well as presents. But where did she get it from? And now Alexandra established a whole system of espionage upon the unsuspecting Maria Vasiljevna.

The penknife was only the last link in a long chain of evidence. The story proved to be more interesting than anybody had expected. Njania was suddenly seized with the detective mania, which often slumbers in old women; besides, on this occasion she was stirred by the feeling how deeply she had wronged Fekluscha, and she was very anxious to repair the evil she had done. For this reason she and Alexandra concluded a solemn offensive and defensive alliance against Maria Vasiljevna. As both were fully convinced of her guilt, they did not hesitate to go to the extremity of secretly taking her keys, and watching for the first opportunity when she was out to search her drawers.

No sooner said than done. Alas, the result showed that their suspicions were only too just. The contents of the drawers proved beyond doubt, that the miserable Maria Vasiljevna was guilty of all the thefts that had created such a sensation of late.

'The shameless creature! to go and bribe poor Fekluscha with jam in order to throw suspicion on her! what an ungodly wretch, not to have the slightest pity on the child!' Njania exclaimed horror stricken, and quite forgetting the part she had played herself in the story—that it was her own hardness which had pushed the girl to accuse herself falsely.

We can imagine the general's fury when this painful truth came to light.

In his first flash of anger, Ivan Sergejevitsch meant to send for the police, and to have Maria

Vasiljevna arrested; but considering her weak health, that she was not young, and moreover, that she had been an inmate of the house for so long, he had mercy on her, and contented himself with giving her notice, and ordering her to be sent away to St Petersburg.

Maria Vasiljevna ought to have been satisfied with this sentence, we should have thought. She was so clever with her needle that there was not the slightest reason for her to be afraid of starving in St Petersburg. Besides, what would her position be with the Rajevskis after such a scandal? All the other servants had been jealous of her, and hated her for her pride. This she knew, and she was also well aware that she would have to pay for her former arrogance. Nevertheless, strange as it may seem, she was not at all satisfied with the general's sentence, and she kept imploring him to have mercy on her.

She seemed to have attached herself to the house with a kind of feline affection, and to cling to the room in which she had lived so long.

'I shan't live many years longer,' she said, I feel that I shall die soon; do they want me to spend my last moments among strangers?'

However, Njania felt sure that this was not

N

the real reason. She could not make up her mind to leave the house, as long as Philip Matvjejitsch remained there, for she well knew that, when once she was gone, she would never see him again. And of course she must be madly in love with him, or else she who had been an honest girl all her life would not for his sake have committed such a sin.

As for Philip Matvjejitsch, he escaped quite unmolested. Perhaps he told the truth, when he said that he had not had the slightest suspicion whence the gifts came, which he had received from Maria Vasiljevna. At all events, as it was no easy matter to find a good gardener, and, as the park and gardens could not be left to themselves, it was decided that he should remain till further notice.

Whether Njania was right or wrong in her supposition about Maria Vasiljevna's motives, so much is certain, that when the day of departure came, she went up to Ivan Sergejevitsch, and fell on her knees before him.

'Do let me stay here without salary, punish me as if I were a bondwoman, but don't drive me away!' she implored, with tears in her eyes.

Ivan Sergejevitsch felt touched at her attachment to his house, but on the other side, he

was afraid that, if he pardoned her, it would
be demoralising for the other servants.   He was
very doubtful what to do, but suddenly an idea
struck him.

'Yes,' he said, 'though stealing is a great sin,
I should have pardoned you, if you hadn't done
anything else.   But through you, a poor innocent
girl · has suffered cruelly; remember, it was
your fault that Fekluscha had to undergo this
dreadful humiliation of public chastisement.   For
her sake, I cannot forgive you.   So, if you
insist on wishing to remain here, I only consent
on one condition ; that you ask Fekluscha's
pardon, and kiss her hand in presence of all
the servants. If you agree to that, in God's
name you may stay !'

Nobody expected that Maria Vasiljevna would
consent to such a condition.   How should she,
proud as she was, condescend to humiliate
herself publicly before a serf, and kiss her hand
into the bargain?   But to the general surprise
she did consent.

An hour later, the whole household was
gathered in the large entrance hall, in order to
assist at this peculiar spectacle : Maria Vasiljevna
kissing Fekluscha's hand.   The general had
insisted on its being done publicly, in the most

solemn manner. The master and mistress were present, and the children had begged permission to be there also.

Tania could never forget the scene that ensued. Fekluscha, who was quite bewildered at the honour which befell her so unexpectedly, and who at the same time was afraid that Maria Vasiljevna would make her suffer later on for her present humiliation, went up to Ivan Sergejevitsch, and asked him to take back his order about the kiss.

'I will forgive her all the same,' she said, almost crying.

But Ivan Sergejevitsch, who had worked up his mind for the occasion, and who felt convinced that he was acting according to the strictest justice, fired up at her: 'Go away, silly girl, that's no business of yours! It is not for your sake, it is for the sake of the principle, that this must be done. If I had committed this sin against you, I, your master, I should have thought it my duty to kiss your hand. You don't understand—never mind—go away and keep quiet!'

Fekluscha trembled, and dared not say any more; she went to her place like a criminal awaiting his sentence.

White as a sheet, Maria Vasiljevna advanced through the crowd; she walked mechanically, as if in sleep, but her face expressed such firm resolution, such hatred, that it made you shudder. She went straight up to Fekluscha.

'Pardon me!' she burst out—it came like a wail, and she seized Fekluscha's hand, and raised it to her lips so vehemently, as if she was going to bite her. But all of a sudden she was seized by a convulsive fit, and fell to the ground shrieking loudly.

Later on it was known that she had suffered from similar attacks before, but she had taken good care to hide these epileptic fits from her masters, for fear that they might send her away. And those of the servants who had known it, had been discreet enough not to betray her.

Tania never learned what effect the present fit had had upon the spectators, for the children of course were taken away immediately; besides, the excitement very nearly made them hysterical too.

So much the more distinctly did she remember the sudden change that took place in the minds of the servants. Up till now, all had felt angry and hostile towards Maria Vasiljevna; her conduct appeared so mean and shameful, that

they felt a kind of satisfaction in shewing her
their contempt, and in offending her where they
could.   But now it was the reverse; all of a
sudden she had become a suffering victim, the
subject of general sympathy.   There was a secret
protest against Ivan Sergejevitsch's exaggerated
severity.

'Of course she had done wrong,' they admitted,
when gossiping with Njania in the nursery,
which they used to do after all important events.
'If the general himself or her ladyship had
punished her, as they do in other houses, it
wouldn't have been so bad, anybody could put
up with that!   But the idea of making her kiss
the hand of that brat Fekluscha!   Who could
survive such shame?'

It took Maria Vasiljevna a long time to
recover.   Her attacks kept returning at intervals
of a few hours.   A doctor had to be sent for.

Pity for the patient, and anger with the master,
increased among the servants.   Elena Paulovna
came to the nursery where Njania was making
tea at an unusual hour.   'For whom is that,
Njania?' her mistress asked innocently.

'Of course for Maria Vasiljevna.   I suppose
she must be allowed to have a cup of tea when
she is ill?   We servants, at least, have got some

Christian charity,' Njania answered in such a temper, that Elena Paulovna was quite bewildered, and hurried out of the room. And this was Njania, who, a few hours previously, could have almost killed Maria Vasiljevna in her anger!

After a few days, Maria recovered entirely, to everybody's satisfaction, and she continued living with the Rajevskis as before. No more was said about the past, not even among the servants.

As for Tania, ever after that day, she felt a peculiar sympathy with Maria Vasiljevna, mixed with a kind of terror. She did not visit her as before, and when they met in the passage, she involuntarily squeezed herself against the wall, trying not to look at her—she was always afraid that Maria Vasiljevna might fall down and begin to scream.

Maria probably noticed that the child kept aloof from her; and she tried every means to win back her affection. She used to surprise her with little presents: a fine silk rag, a new dress for her doll, etc. But it was no use, the secret terror remained, and Tania ran away as soon as she was left alone with Maria Vasiljevna.

Besides, soon after, she came under the influence of the new governess, who put an end to her intercourse with the servants.

But one Sunday evening, when Tania was
seven or eight years old, she came running
through the passage past Maria Vasiljevna's
room. Suddenly, Maria opened her door, and
said : 'Little Miss! just come in a moment, here
is a beautiful bird of dough I have baked for
you!' It was nearly dark, and the child was
alone with Maria Vasiljevna, whose white face
and large black eyes frightened her so much, that
without answering, she ran away as fast as she
could.

'Oh, I see, Miss Tania despises me!' she
heard Maria mutter to herself. She was struck,
not so much by the words as by the tone in
which they were spoken, but she did not stop.
When she was in the schoolroom, and had recovered a little from her fright, Maria Vasiljevna's
deep sad voice still sounded in her ears. Tania
felt uncomfortable the whole evening, though
she tried to divert her thoughts by playing.
She could not banish Maria Vasiljevna from
her mind. She felt as we often do with regard
to a person we have wronged; Maria had
suddenly become a dear good friend, and Tania
was longing for her.

To tell her governess what had happened was
out of the question ; children are always shy

about their feelings.   Besides, they were not
allowed to mix with the servants, so she might
perhaps even be commended for her conduct,
and she felt instinctively, that she would not
like to be praised for this.   After tea, when the
children were to go to bed, the idea struck her
that she might go and see Maria Vasiljevna,
instead of going straight to her bedroom.   This
was a great sacrifice on her part, for she would
be obliged to run through the long dark passage
quite alone.   But a desperate courage came over
her.   She ran as fast as she could, and like a
hurricane came rushing into Maria's room.

Maria Vasiljevna had had her supper, and as
it was a holiday, she was not at work, but was
sitting at her table, which was covered with a
clean white cloth, reading a religious book.   A
lamp was burning in front of the Saint, and
Tania thought the room was so bright and comfortable, and Maria herself looked so gentle.

' I am coming to say good night, dearest
Maria ! ' Tania burst out breathlessly, but before
she had finished, Maria Vasiljevna clasped her
in her arms, and covered her with kisses, and she
went on caressing her till Tania got quite
frightened, and began to think how she might
escape without wounding Maria's feelings again.

At last a violent fit of coughing obliged Maria to let her go.

This cough became worse and worse. 'I have been barking the whole night,' she used to say, with a kind of gloomy irony. And day by day she looked paler and more transparent, but she persistently refused to consult a doctor; besides, it always made her cross to be talked to about her illness.

In this way she lived on a few years longer. She took to her bed only two days before her death, but her last struggle was very hard and painful.

The general ordered a stately funeral for her, at which the whole household assisted. Even Fekluscha followed her to the grave, with streaming tears.

Only Philip Matvjejitsch was missing. Without waiting for her death, he had left the Rajevskis some time previously, in order to accept another more profitable engagement.

III

CHANGES

THE uncomfortable episode with Maria Vasilevna was the prelude to a series of complica-
tions which induced Ivan Sergejevitsch to devote
some attention to the nursery, in which, up to
that time, he had had very little too.

Ivan Sergejevitsch made the unexpected discovery that his children were by no means so
exemplary in their conduct as he had fancied.

For example, one day the two girls went out
alone, and lost their way, so that they were not
found till the evening, and then they had eaten
poisonous berries, which made them ill the next
day. This event showed, to begin with, that
there was great negligence in the way the children were superintended, and this discovery was
rapidly followed by others.

Up till now, Aniuta had been supposed to be
phenomenally above her age in cleverness ; now

it appeared that she was not only dreadfully
spoilt, but exceedingly ignorant for a girl of
twelve; she could not even write her own language properly.

And worst of all, it came to light that the
French governess was given to a vice so ugly
that it could not be mentioned in the children's
presence.

A sad time followed; Tania remembered it
dimly afterwards as a kind of general domestic
misery. In the nursery there was nothing but
rows and tears. All quarrelled, all were scolded,
the innocent as well as the guilty. The father
was in a temper, the mother in tears. Njania
cried, the French governess was wringing her
hands and packing up her things. Tania and
Aniuta dared not stir, for they were the scape-
goats on whom all vented their tempers; and
the slightest wrong was treated as a crime. At
the same time, they felt a kind of curious interest
in what was going on, and in listening to the
quarrels amongst their elders, wondering what
would be the end of it all.

Ivan Sergejevitsch, who did not like half-
measures, made up his mind that the whole
educational system was to be thoroughly
reformed. The French governess got notice,

Njania was dismissed from the nursery, and was made superintendent of the linen department; and two new persons made their appearance : a Polish tutor and an English governess.

The tutor proved to be a worthy man, who understood his business thoroughly, but, truth to tell, he had no influence on the children's education. The governess, on the contrary, introduced quite a new element into the house.

Though she was born in Russia, and spoke Russian fluently, she had retained the typical Anglo-Saxon qualities—honesty and perseverance. As this last characteristic did not belong to the family, it explains the great influence she came to exercise on her surroundings.

All her first efforts were directed to a complete reform of the nursery, where she wanted to bring up her pupils as exemplary English girls.

Heaven knows, it was no easy task to establish an English system in a noble Russian family, with its century-old habits of laziness, carelessness, and despotism.

Nevertheless, owing to her wonderful tenacity, she attained her end to a certain extent.

Not with Aniuta, however, whose habits of unlimited freedom were too inveterate. They spent a few years together amidst incessant

skirmishes, till Aniuta was fifteen, when, once
for all, she withdrew her allegiance from the
governess. The outward token of Aniuta's
emancipation was that her bed was moved from
the nursery to a room adjoining Elena Paulovna's. From that day, Aniuta considered herself ' grown up and out,' and the governess seized
every opportunity of asserting that Aniuta's
behaviour did not concern her any more, and
that she had renounced all responsibility for it.

She now devoted her whole attention to
Tania, whom she isolated from the rest of the
family, and tried to protect from her elder sister's
influence as anxiously as if she was guarding her
against the pestilence. And this system of ex-
clusion was facilitated by the arrangement of the
house, where two or three families might have
lived easily, without incommoding each other in
the least.

Nearly the whole ground-floor, except a few
spare rooms and some of the servants' rooms, was
left to the governess and Tania. The drawing-
room floor, with the elegantly furnished reception
rooms, belonged to Elena Paulovna and Aniuta.
Fedia and his tutor had one wing, and the
general's study occupied the ground-floor of a
tower, which formed a building by itself, separate

from the house. So the different groups of the Rajevski family had each their territory, and had no need to interfere with each other. Only at the two meals, dinner, and tea in the evening. the whole circle was united.

IV

EDUCATION

A STRICTLY regulated life had begun for Tania. She shared her bedroom with her governess, who superintended her dressing, made her get up at seven and take a cold bath in the morning. Though Tania did not like this process she felt very comfortable after it, and generally began her day in high spirits; but her gay humour was soon checked by Malvina Jakov-levna, who suffered from her liver, and was seldom cheerful in the morning. After break-fast, work invariably began with a music lesson. An hour and a half of scales and exercises was not very cheering either. So long as Aniuta shared the lessons, Tania took great inerest in them; she listened attentively, and frequently remembered the whole lesson when her elder sister had forgotten everything. But though she was still fairly industrious, her studies had lost all attraction for her.

They had lunch at twelve, and as soon as the last mouthful was swallowed, the governess went to the window and examined the weather. If the thermometer showed less than ten degrees below freezing-point, and if there was no wind, they would walk for an hour and a half up and down the alley which had been cleared from snow, but if it was very cold and windy Malvina Jakovlevna would take her indispensable walk by herself, and Tania was sent to one of the large rooms up stairs, where she had to play with her ball.

Tania did not care very much for this occupation, still she gladly obeyed the order, as it gave her an hour and a half to herself. During these hours her imagination would work freely ; she recited the poems she knew by heart, or others which she invented herself. She was very fond of poetry, and felt convinced that she would become a poet herself. In fact, from her fifth year she had tried to write verses, but this exercise was not to the taste of her governess, who had cruelly ridiculed her attempts, and done her best to stop them.

Adjoining the large hall where Tania took

her exercise, when she was alone, was the library, which proved a great temptation. Here books lay scattered on tables, chairs, and sofas, and there was the greatest variety of foreign novels and Russian periodicals. Tania was strictly forbidden to touch any of these books, for Malvina Jakovlevna was most particular about her reading, and did not allow her pupil to read anything she did not know thoroughly herself; but as she read rather slowly, and seldom found time to peruse such books as the child wished to have, Tania was in a chronic state of mental hunger. How then could she be expected always to resist the forbidden fruit?

She would struggle for a few moments, then take one of the books in her hand, and read a few lines here and there, and again run back to the hall and play for a while; but at last the temptation was too strong, and so by degrees one book was read after the other. Now and then she rushed into the other room and played with the ball, and so she generally escaped discovery. But occasionally she would be so absorbed in her reading that she forgot the time, and was caught in the very act by her governess, and this entailed the worst punishment Tania knew: she was sent to her father, to confess her misdeed to him herself.

Ivan Sergejevitsch was by no means severe with his children, but he seldom saw them, and there was no familiarity between them, except when they were ill. Then he used to be quite a different person—the fear of losing them would dominate all other feelings. His voice and whole manner became so kind and gentle; he would caress them and play with them better than anybody else. And at such times the children idolised their father, and fondly cherished the memory of his kindness. But as soon as they were all right again he thought he ought to resume his severity, and was very sparing of his caresses.

He liked solitude and lived in his own world, to which nobody was admitted. Not even Elena Paulovna entered his sanctuary without knocking, and the children would never have dared to come unbidden.

So the governess's order, 'Go to your father and confess!' was the most awful sentence for Tania; but it was no use crying and resisting; a firm hand took hold of her and dragged her to the general's door, where she was left to her fate. There stands Ilia, her father's valet, with the most irritating smile on his face; she cannot go back to the schoolroom without adding open disobedience to her transgression; on the other hand, it is unbearable to stand there exposed to the servant's pity or mockery. so there is nothing left but to knock at the door and face her father's anger. She knocks feebly.

'Louder, Miss,' says the intolerable Ilia, who seems to enjoy the scene thoroughly.

She knocks again.

'Who is there? come in!' a voice answers.

Tania enters, but stops just inside the door.

Her father is sitting at the writing-table with his back towards the door.

'Well, what's the matter? who is it?' he exclaims impatiently.

'It is I, Malvina Jakovlevna has sent me,' Tania answers with a sob.

Now Ivan Sergejevitsch knows what is the matter. 'Oh, I see, you have been playing your pranks again,' he says, trying to speak harshly. 'Well, what's it about?' And with streaming tears Tania falters out her confession. Ivan Sergejevitsch does not listen very attentively. His pedagogical ideas are most elementary; he thinks education is women's business, and of

course he has not the remotest idea of the
complicated feelings of the little girl who stands
there awaiting her doom ; to him she is still the
little Tania of five years ago. Evidently he is
in great doubt what to do on this occasion.
Her transgression does not seem of great
consequence to him, but he firmly believes that
severity is necessary in education. In his own
mind he feels rather vexed with the governess
for not being able to settle this simple affair by
herself; but as he has been appealed to in the
matter, of course he must show his paternal
authority, and so he looks very severe.

'You are a naughty, disobedient girl, and I
am very cross with you,' he says, and then makes
a pause because he does not know what to say.
'Go and put yourself in a corner,' he orders at
last ; for of all wise pedagogical rules, one only
has fastened itself in his memory, that naughty
children are to stand in the corner of disgrace.

And Tania, a girl of twelve, who a few moments
ago has passed through the most exciting
psychological scenes with the heroine of the
novel she has been reading, must go and stand
in a corner like a silly baby !

Ivan Sergejevitsch resumes his work. There
is deep silence in the room ; Tania stands

motionless, but a torrent of conflicting feelings pour in upon her during these minutes. She sees clearly how useless and silly this punishment is, but a kind of shame makes her submit to it in silence, without tears or complaints, though resentment at the bitter wrong she is suffering, and her powerlessness against it, threaten to choke her. And to add to her torture, in comes the valet, who has found a pretext for entering the room, on purpose, of course, to see her punishment.

Her father seems to have forgotten all about it, but at last he remembers her, and sends her away, saying : ' Well, you may go now, but don't do it again !' Perhaps he would have been horrified if he had been able to look into the child's heart. Tania leaves his room with a grief far beyond her years, and with a feeling of humiliation so bitter, that only twice since, in the darkest hours of her life, has she had similar feelings.

She returns to the schoolroom, silent and subdued. Her governess is satisfied with the result of her method of education, and for several days afterwards Tania is so quiet and submissive, that no fault can be found with her conduct. But Malvina Jakovlevna would be less pleased if she knew the impression this event had left in the girl's mind.

The conviction that she was not loved by her family went like a dark thread through all Tania's recollections from her childhood. It had been nourished by accidental remarks of the servants, and it increased throughout the solitary life she led with her governess.

Malvina Jakovlevna's lot was not very cheerful either. Plain, alone in the world, no longer young, a stranger in Russia, where she never felt quite at home, and longing for English surroundings, she concentrated on Tania all the devotion of which her stiff, energetic, and anything but sentimental nature was capable. Elena Paulovna and the governess were two so opposite natures, that sympathy between them was impossible.

In character, as well as in outward appearance, Tania's mother was one of those women who never grow old. She was of noble German extraction, but her family had lived many years in Russia. Her grandfather had been a well-known man of science, and her father was the chief of the Military Academy. His position gave him access to the highest circles in St Petersburg, military as well as scientific, and he received in his home the élite of society. His wife had died early, but his numerous unmarried sisters lived with him, and superintended his household.

Consequently, Elena Paulovna, as a young girl, never came into contact with the practical side of life. She got a better education than most Russian girls at that time, played the piano very well, sang admirably, spoke several foreign languages, and had a pretty good knowledge of French and German literature. Moreover, she had artistic tastes, though none of her gifts were so prominent as to call for great sacrifices on her part, nor did they interfere with the tastes and habits of her surroundings. On the contrary, she cultivated her talents more for the pleasure of others than for her own sake.

The guests in her father's house had mostly been elderly, serious people, who were fond of the fine clever girl, and liked to chat with her; they had looked upon her and treated her as a child; and so did her husband, who was much older than she.

Ivan Sergejevitsch was a widower when he married Elena Paulovna, but he had no children by his first wife. If Elena had married into a German family, she might have become an excellent mistress of the house, but in her Russian home it was rather difficult to develop domestic virtues. The order of this house was maintained as it had been for generations in the Rajevski family. The servants were old serfs, and had long ago arrogated all power and authority; and their new mistress, who was almost a child, and of a gentle, yielding disposition, could not assert herself sufficiently to carry out any change in the household. In the few cases in which she had attempted an innovation, her orders had been carried out so reluctantly, and with such evident intention to do wrong, that after all, poor Elena Paulovna had been obliged to acknowledge her deficiency, and with every defeat, of course, the servants' tyranny had increased.

She was simply afraid of the governess, who, on her side, treated the young mistress somewhat harshly, and considered herself the sovereign in the children's room. Consequently Elena seldom went to the schoolroom, and never interfered with her children's education.

As for Tania, she adored her mother, and thought her the finest, most lovely of all the women she knew; but she could not help feeling a little wronged by her—why did her mother love her less than her sister and brother?

It is evening; Tania sits in the schoolroom; she has finished her lessons for to-morrow, but her governess has kept her back on purpose, as she does not want her to go and join the others. She hears music from the drawing-room. Elena Paulovna generally plays on the piano of an evening; she knows a great deal of music by heart, and can go on for hours with her improvisations from one tune to another. It is Tania's great delight to listen to her mother's playing. At last she is allowed to escape, and rushes up stairs. When she enters the drawing-room, Elena Paulovna has stopped playing, and sits on the sofa with Aniuta and Fedia, one on each side, clinging to her. They are chatting and laughing, and don't take any notice of Tania at all. She joins them for a few moments, hoping to attract their attention, but in vain. She feels a chill in her heart; 'they enjoy themselves better without me,' is her bitter thought, and instead of covering her mother's delicate hands with kisses, as she had been longing to do, she retires to a remote corner, and keeps sulking till the party is called in to tea, whereupon she has to go to bed.

V

UNCLE PETER SERGEJEVITSCH

Two persons became the object of Tania's warm attachment, her father's eldest brother, and her mother's only brother. The former, Peter Sergejevitsch Rajevski, was a very tall, stately old man, with a large head and beautiful white wavy hair. His face, with its fine regular profile, grey bushy brows, and deep perpendicular furrow dividing the forehead, would have looked almost fierce, but for a pair of kind, honest, and innocent eyes, such as we frequently see in faces of small children or Newfoundland dogs.

Peter Sergejevitsch was no worldly-wise man. Though he was the eldest son, and ought to have been the head of the family, everybody had treated him like a big baby. He was very original, and a dreamer. His wife was dead, and he had left his considerable fortune to their only son, reserving a small allowance for himself.

He frequently visited his brother at Palibino, and would remain for weeks. The arrival was hailed as a festival by the children, and his presence always made the house more bright and cheerful.

His favourite room was the library, where he would sit the whole day without stirring from the large leather sofa, quite absorbed in the *Revue des deux Mondes*, his favourite reading.

In fact, reading was his only mania; he took great interest in politics, and devoured the newspapers that came once a week; he would brood over them for hours, wondering what new villanies Napoleon would commit, and worrying himself a good deal about Bismarck too. He felt convinced that Napoleon would make havoc with the Germans in the end, and as he did not live to see 1870, he died in this conviction.

In politics, Peter Sergejevitsch was dreadfully bloodthirsty. To massacre an army of a hundred thousand men seemed a mere trifle to him. In theory, he was equally merciless in punishing criminals, though in real life he took all men to be good and honest.

He had frequent skirmishes with the governess, whom he irritated by saying that all the English

governors of India ought to have been hanged.
'Yes, yes, Miss, every one of them!' he would
burst out passionately, banging the table with
his fist.   Anybody seeing him at such a moment
would have been frightened to death.   But then
he would suddenly calm down and look quite
distressed, finding that his violent gestures had
awakened the greyhound Grisi, who was just
taking a nap on the sofa.

But nothing gave Peter Sergejevitsch more
delight than to read about new scientific dis-
coveries.   He would tell all about them at
dinner, and on these occasions the conversation
became lively, and frequently very aggressive.
As a rule, there was silence at meals, because
the persons present did not share one another's
interests, and so had nothing to talk about.

'Have you read about Paul Bert's new
invention?' Peter Sergejevitsch asks, and gives
an account of the article he has read, with
unconscious exaggerations of the facts, and
drawing conclusions as to their importance
and consequences, which are so bold that they
would most likely have surpassed the inventor's
wildest dreams.   Hot arguments follow.   Elena
Paulovna and Aniuta, as a rule, join in Peter
Sergejevitsch's enthusiasm; the governess almost

as invariably takes the opposite view, and begins a violent attack on the theories advocated by Peter Sergejevitsch, declaring them to be false. if not criminal. The Polish tutor now and then raises his voice to correct some formal detail, though he wisely abstains from any active part in the discussion. As for Ivan Sergejevitsch, he represents critical scepticism, and does not side with either of the parties, contenting himself with discovering and pointing out the weak points in both camps.

The discussions sometimes assume a very warlike character. By some unfortunate chance they invariably end in petty personal attacks. The hottest opponents are always Malvina Jakovlevna and Aniuta, whose five years' feud is only interrupted by short periods of armed peace.

If Peter Sergejevitsch draws the boldest general conclusions from isolated facts, the governess on her side is not less ingenious in using the contrary method. In discussing the most abstract scientific theories, she will find astonishing opportunities for blaming Aniuta's conduct, and her arguments seem so unwarranted, that you are taken completely aback.

Aniuta does not hang back, and her answers are so malicious and impudent, that the governess rises from table in high dudgeon, declaring that after such insults she can remain in the house no longer. Everybody, of course, feels uncomfortable ; Elena Paulovna, who hates scenes and quarrels, undertakes the part of a mediator, and after long negotiations peace is restored at last.

Tania particularly remembers the hurricane caused by two articles in the *Revue des deux Mondes*, one by Professor Helmholtz about the 'unity of physical powers,' the other by Claude Bernard about experiments with pigeons' brains. No doubt the two learned professors would have been much surprised had they been told what bones of contention they had thrown into an inoffensive Russian family, living in the remote province of Vitebsk.

Peter Sergejevitsch was also fond of reading novels, travels, and historical essays, and would even condescend to children's books. We should have thought that he, a wealthy Russian landowner, might easily have satisfied this innocent passion by collecting a library for himself, but as a fact he scarcely possessed a book, and it was not till late in life that the Palibino library offered him an opportunity of revelling in his favourite occupation.

The weakness of character which formed such a striking contrast to his stately martial appearance, had always made him the victim of others, and he had never allowed himself to satisfy any personal inclinations.

On account of this deficiency, his parents had not thought him fit for the military career, which in his youth was considered the only suitable position for a nobleman ; but they had decided to keep him at home, and let him have just as much education as would enable him not to sink to the level of a rough country squire. Whatever knowledge he possessed beyond these first elements he had himself acquired ; and he had considerable reading, though of a desultory kind, being very well grounded in some subjects, and very defective in others, like most self-taught people. He continued to live with his parents, accepting his humble position without the slightest resentment or dissatisfaction.

His younger and cleverer brothers patronised him in a good-natured, inoffensive, way, and looked upon him as an eccentric.

But suddenly the most unexpected thing happened. Nadeschda Andrejevna N., the greatest beauty and the richest heiress in the government (county), honoured him with her attention. Whether she was captivated by his person, or whether she had simply made out that he was exactly the husband she wanted, whom she would like to see always at her feet, as her obedient and loving giant—she showed distinctly that she was ready to accept him as her husband.

Peter Sergejevitsch would never have dared to dream of such a thing ; but a host of aunts and sisters hastened to inform him of this marvellous chance, and before he had time to realise the fact, he was betrothed to the beautiful, rich, and spoiled Nadeschda Andrejevna.

But their married life was not happy.

Though the children at Palibino firmly believed that Uncle Peter existed only for their private pleasure, and though they chatted freely to him about everything else, they felt instinctively that there was one subject they were never to mention—his late wife.

They had heard awful stories about Aunt Nadeschda Andrejevna, though neither from their parents nor their governess, who never mentioned her name in their presence. But their youngest unmarried aunt, Anna Sergejevna, used to have a gossiping fit now and then, and she had told the children terrible things about their late aunt.

P

'You have no idea what a snake she was, and the life she led your Aunt Marpha and myself! And poor brother Peter, he had his fill of her too! When she was angry with one of the servants, for instance, she would rush into his room, and ask him to punish the culprit with his own hand. Of course, he was much too kind-hearted to do that, and he would try to reason with her,—no use! she only flew into a rage, and showered abuse on him. And he—old woman as he was—would sit and listen in silence. At last, seeing that she could not rouse his temper with her words, she would take his papers and books, in fact, everything she could get hold of, and fling it into the fire, exclaiming: "I won't have that old rubbish in my house!" Occasionally she would even pull off her slipper and give him a box on the ear! And he, silly thing, what did he do? He tried to take her hands—very careful not to hurt her—and said, as gently as possible: "What's the matter with you, Nadenka? Try to control yourself; are you not ashamed to behave like this?"

'But she did'nt mind in the least?'

'How could he stand it? why did'nt he try to get rid of her?' the children exclaimed, flushing with indignation.

'Oh, well, a husband can't throw off his wife like an old glove,' Anna Sergejevna answered; 'besides, I must say, that though she treated him badly, he loved her dearly all the same.'

'But how could he? such a Xantippe!'

'He did love her, anyhow, and he could not live without her. When they had done away with her, he grieved so deeply, that he very nearly put an end to his own life.'

'What do you mean, auntie? You say they did away with her?' the children asked, in the greatest excitement.

Auntie, who feels that she has said too much, suddenly falls silent, and knits fast at her stocking, to show that she is not going to say any more.

But the children's curiosity is roused, and they don't give in.

'Oh, *do* tell us, auntie dear,' they beseech.

And, perhaps, Anna Sergejevna feels rather a temptation to go on, as she has told so much of the story.

'Well, her own servants did it,' she suddenly answers.

'Oh, how dreadful! How did they do it?'

'It was this way,' Anna Sergejevna begins again: 'One night she was alone, having sent

Uncle Peter and the children away.   Her maid
and favourite, Malanga, undressed her as usual,
and helped her to bed ; but then she claps her
hands three times, and on this signal the other
maid-servants rush into the room, as well as
Fedor, the coachman, and Yevstignej, the
gardener.   Nadeschda Andrejevna sees the
danger, but she does not show any fear, nor lose
her presence of mind : " What ever do you want
here, rascals ? Are you mad ? Will you go away
instantly ! "   And so strong was the force of
habit, that they hesitated and began to retire,
when Malanga, the boldest of them, stopped
them, and cried out : " Cowards, what are you
thinking of ?   Aren't you afraid ?   Don't you
see that she will send us to Siberia to-morrow ? "
Then they took courage, and rushed up to her
bed ; some seized her hands, others her feet ;
they heaped pillows and eiderdowns on the top
of her, to suffocate her.   She screamed and implored them to spare her, promising money
and everything else if they would allow her to
live. But no ; they were not to be bribed. And
Malanga, her favourite, told them to put a wet
towel on her head, to prevent blue spots appearing on her face.

' Afterwards, they freely confessed their deed,

the stupid slaves, and gave a detailed report to the judge of what had happened. And dearly they had to pay for it. They were flogged, and sent to Siberia, where many of them are still dragging on a miserable existence.'

Aunt Anna stops, and the children are horror-stricken.

'Now, you must not for the world let your parents know what I have told you,' she says; and the children feel perfectly well that it would'nt do to speak to their parents or governess about these things; it would make a dreadful scene, and they would never be told anything again.

But Tania is haunted by this awful story, and cannot sleep for it.

Once, when visiting her uncle, she had seen a full-length portrait in oil of Nadeschda Andrejevna, painted in the conventional fashion; and now, all of a sudden, this picture stands vividly before her—this doll-like lady with the small and delicate limbs, in a low red velvet dress, with a garnet necklace on her plump white neck, full, rosy cheeks, proud, large, black eyes, and a stereotyped smile about her tiny, red mouth. And Tania pictures to herself the wild horror in those eyes, when she suddenly saw her own serfs rush into the room to take her life.

Whenever she is alone with her uncle this story is present to her mind, and she is quite at a loss to understand how this man, who has experienced such awful things, can be so calm and cheerful now, as if nothing had happened ; that he can play chess with her, make paper boats, and fire up at an article in the paper. Now and then she feels a morbid desire to speak to her uncle about the forbidden subject ; she will sit staring at him, trying to imagine this tall, strong and wise man, trembling before this little beauty of a wife, weeping and kissing her hands while she tears his books and papers, and takes off her little slipper to box his ears. Once, and once only, was the temptation too strong for her to resist.

It was evening, and they were alone in the library ; her uncle was sitting on the sofa, as usual, reading a book ; Tania was playing with her ball ; at last she got tired, and sat down on the sofa beside him, leaning her head on his shoulder, and her thoughts took the usual turn.

Peter Sergejevitsch put down his book, passed his hand over her hair, and said kindly, 'What is my little girl thinking of so deeply ? '

' Uncle, weren't you very unhappy with your wife ? ' Tania bursts out almost involuntarily.

She never forgot the effect of that unexpected
question on poor Peter Sergejevitsch.   His calm
features were contracted as in physical pain, and
he stretched out his hands as if to avert a blow.
Tania felt the intensest pity and shame—it was
almost as if she had boxed his ears with a
slipper.

'Dear, darling uncle, forgive me!   I did'nt
know what I was saying!' she whispered, clinging to him, and hiding her flushed face on his
bosom.   And her kind-hearted uncle had to
comfort her for her untimely curiosity.

Of course, Tania never again returned to the
forbidden subject, but she talked to him freely
about everything else. She used to be his special
favourite, and they would sit together talking for
hours.   When his head was full of some meta-
physical idea, he could neither think nor speak
of anything else; and when he had no other
listeners, he would expound his abstract theories
to Tania, quite forgetting that she was a child.

But this was exactly what she liked, and she
exerted herself to the utmost to understand him,
or at least to pretend that she did.

Though Peter Sergejevitsch had never studied
mathematics properly, he had the deepest veneration for this science, and had gathered some scraps

of knowledge here and there; he liked to discuss mathematical problems, and would frequently do so in Tania's presence. It was he who first talked to her about squaring the circle. Of course, she did not understand anything, but she was deeply impressed with this wonderful mystical science, that seemed to open to its adepts a world of miracles inaccessible to the uninitiated. Another rather peculiar circumstance had awakened her interest for mathematics.

One of the walls in a room which was to be repapered, had an intermediate covering of old sheets of paper, which were full of mathematical designs, dating from the time when Ivan Sergejevitsch had studied this science in his youth. These mysterious lines soon attracted Tania's curiosity; she would stand looking at them for hours, and try to find the order in which the sheets ought to have been put together. So by degrees a number of formulas fastened themselves in her memory; even the text seemed to impress itself on her brain, though she did not catch its meaning.

When many years later, in St Petersburg, as a girl of fifteen, she took her first lessons in differential calculus, her teacher was surprised to find how quickly she understood and remembered mathematical problems, as though she had studied them before.   And so she had, indeed ; the moment he explained them to her, the real meaning dawned upon her of the words and formulas which had long been stowed away in some recess of her brain.

VI

UNCLE FEDOR PAULITSCH

TANIA'S attachment to her maternal uncle was of a very different nature. He was her mother's only brother, and much younger than she. He lived in St. Petersburg, and being the only male heir to the distinguished old name, he was idolised by his sisters and numerous aunts, all unmarried women.

It was a great event at Palibino when he came on a visit. Tania was nine years old when he came for the first time. For weeks nothing else had been talked of, the best spare room was put in order to receive him, and a carriage was sent to fetch him from the county town, about 100 miles from Palibino. But the day before he was expected, a simple telega pulled up before the door, and out jumped a young man in a light overcoat with a travelling bag on his

shoulders, and the family rushed out into the
hall to meet him.

Fedor Paulitsch had a pleasant voice; he
seemed quite young, his short chestnut hair
stood like a velvet cushion round his head, his
cheeks were flushed with the cold air, his bright
brown eyes looked round merrily, he had a
fine moustache, and from between his fresh
red lips a set of brilliant white teeth shone
out.

'How beautiful! how stately!' Tania thought,
and kept looking at him in rapture.

'Who is that? Aniuta?' he asked pointing at
Tania.

'Oh dear no; what are you thinking of, Fedia?
Aniuta is quite a young lady; this is only Tania,'
Elena Paulovna answered in an injured tone.

'Well, your girls are grown indeed! Look
out, Lena, they will soon make an old woman of
you,' Fedor Paulitsch exclaimed laughing, and
kissed Tania. She felt shy without knowing
why, and blushed deeply.

Dinner was very gay; Uncle Fedor kept
chatting the whole time and made everybody
laugh. Ivan Sergejevitsch himself treated his
brother-in-law with great consideration, not in
the patronising way which he sometimes adopted

with the younger men of the family, and which irritated them very much.

Tania could not keep her eyes off him; she admired everything about him, his fine white hands and his smart English suit.

'Do you know, Lena,' he says laughingly to his sister, 'I have been wondering all the time what Tania's eyes are like. Now I have found it out—they look like preserved gooseberries, large, green, and sweet.'

All burst out laughing, and Tania blushed and felt a little bit hurt; but her uncle added, 'Very sweet and very green,' and so she was comforted.

After dinner, her uncle sat down on a corner sofa and took Tania on his knees.

'Now, you come here, we must be friends,' he says, and begins talking about her lessons. Children as a rule are well aware of their strong points, and Tania knows that she possesses very good knowledge for her age, so she is glad that her uncle has chosen this topic; she gives good answers, and he is very much pleased.

'What a sensible little girl you are! That's nice,—you know something, I see!' he keeps saying.

'Now, Uncle, you tell me something,' Tania begs.

'Oh yes, with pleasure; but I suppose such a
lady as you are does not want nursery-tales,'
he says jokingly; 'I shall have to tell you something serious.'   And he begins talking about
coral-reefs, sea-weeds, infusories, etc.   It is very
interesting, and he is quite charmed to see how
eagerly the child listens to these things.

And these delightful tête-à-têtes were resumed
every evening when Ivan Sergejevitsch and Elena
Paulovna had retired for half an hour's nap.
Aniuta and Fedia did not care to listen to these
instructive conversations, and so Tania had her
uncle all to herself, which was the greatest treat
to her.

Now it happened during one of his visits to
Palibino, that a gentleman from the neighbourhood came on a visit with his daughter Olga.
She was the only girl of the same age as herself
with whom Tania had any intercourse.   She did
not come very often, but when she came she used
to remain the whole day, and sometimes all night
too.   She was a lively child, and Tania used to
look forward to her visits.   But this time Tania's
first thought was: 'What is she going to do after
dinner, and how am I to have uncle to myself?'
She felt instinctively that Olga's presence would
spoil the fun, so she received her friend much

less cordially than usual. The whole morning
she kept hoping that Olga would leave early;
but no, she was to stay till late in the evening.
What was to be done? At last she took courage
and spoke openly to her friend.

'Look here, Olga,' she said in her insinuating
way, 'I will play with you the whole day, and
do everything you like; but then you must be
good and leave me alone after dinner. I always
have a little talk with my uncle, and we don't
want you.'

Olga consented readily, and Tania kept faith-
fully her part of the engagement. At last dinner
came. Tania was on tenter-hooks all the time.
'Would Olga keep her promise?' she wondered,
casting eager glances at her friend, and trying to
remind her of her promise by all kinds of signals.

'Well, dearie, what are we going to talk about
to-day?' Fedor Paulitsch asked after dinner,
chucking his little niece affectionately under the
chin. Tania was delighted, clasped his hands,
and was just going to retire to the dear corner
with him, when she suddenly discovered that the
faithless Olga was coming after them. Very likely
if Tania had not said anything at all, Olga would
have been the first to retire on hearing the two
talk about serious matters, for she hated any-

thing that reminded her of lessons; but seeing
Tania's eagerness, she fancied something very
amusing must be going on, and she wanted to
know what it was. 'May I come too?' she in-
quired, looking at Fedor Paulitsch with her fine
eyes.

'Certainly, dear child,' he answered, looking
kindly at her pretty little face.

Tania looked daggers, but Olga was not in the
least affected.

'Olga doesn't know anything about it, she
won't understand,' Tania objected discontentedly.

'Well, then, we must talk about something
else which she likes to hear,' Uncle Fedor replied good-naturedly, taking both little girls by
the hand. Tania was very black; this was not
what she wanted at all; she felt as if she had
been deprived of a treasure which was hers by
right.

'Well, Tania, come along and sit down here
on my lap,' her uncle said, evidently not
noticing her bad humour; but Tania felt very
injured, and this proposal did not soothe her.

'No, I won't,' she answered vehemently, and
squeezed herself into the corner, where she remained sulking. The uncle looked at her with
an astonished smile. Did he suspect the jealousy

that raged in her heart, and was he going to make fun of it? Anyhow, he suddenly turned to Olga and said :

'Very well, Olga, as Tania does not want to come, you sit up here.'

This was an unexpected blow to Tania; she was too much taken aback to protest, and could only stare in silence at her happy rival, who was sitting on her uncle's knee enjoying herself, and quite flushed with excitement.

At last—Tania did not know how it came, it was as if somebody had given her a push—she rushed forward and plunged her teeth into Olga's white arm just above the elbow.

The attack was so sudden, that neither of the three could say anything; they stared at each other for some moments. At last Olga gave a shriek, which roused them to consciousness.

Tania felt deeply ashamed, and ran out of the room. 'You nasty, wicked girl!' her uncle cried angrily after her.

Her constant resort in all her childish griefs was her former nurse, dear old Njania; and with her she sought relief now. Hiding her face in Njania's lap, she had a good long cry, No questions were asked; the old woman only kept patting her head, muttering, 'Poor darling, now be quiet, my own little girl !' And Tania felt a great relief in pouring out her despair to this faithful friend.

Fortunately her governess was out, so nobody missed her. At last Njania gave her a cup of tea and took her to bed, where she soon fell into a heavy sleep.

Next morning she felt dreadfully ashamed, and thought she could never look anybody in the face again. But things went better than she expected. Olga had left in the evening, and had evidently been generous enough not to complain of Tania. Nobody scolded or scoffed at her ; her uncle did not show any change in his manner.

But, strange to say, from that day Tania's feelings towards him were quite changed. They had no more chats in the evening, and he returned to St. Petersburg shortly afterwards. Though he came frequently, and was always very kind to Tania, and though she continued to be fond of him, the idolatrous attachment she had felt towards him was gone for ever.

VII

RURAL PLEASURES.

THE country round Palibino was very wild and much more picturesque than the other parts of Central Russia. The government of Vitebsk is noted for its vast pine-woods and its wealth of beautiful lakes. The spurs of the Waldai-Heights cover part of the country, which consequently looks rugged and hilly compared with the endless plains of which Russia mainly consists. There are scarcely any rocks, but now and then a large granite block surprises you in the midst of a flat tract of country or of a marsh covered with grass six feet high.

Palibino lay quite close to a wood, which gradually became denser and denser, and at last merged into the enormous imperial forest, which extended for hundreds of miles. In its thickets you never heard the sound of an axe, except perhaps at night, when a peasant was bold enough to steal a little crown-wood.

Many curious stories were told about this forest. Of course superstition peopled it with supernatural beings: fairies, trolls and gnomes; and rumours went abroad that it was the resort of thieves, robbers and runaway soldiers. Of wild animals, wolves, bears and lynxes, no doubt there were plenty, and most of the peasants could boast of having seen some of them at least once in their lives.

The English governess at Palibino, who was passionately fond of walking, at first despised all the stories about the wood with which they tried to frighten her; but one autumn day when she was walking with her pupils a couple of miles from the manor, she heard a rustling sound among the trees, and caught sight of a bear with its two young ones crossing the road at some distance. So she became more cautious in future, and never went to the forest unless she had some servants with her.

This forest, however, contained not only horrors and mysteries—it was an inexhaustible store-house of all kinds of treasures. There was an abundance of game—hares, black and hazel grouse, partridges, etc.; great varieties of fruits— strawberries, raspberries, bilberries, cranberries; plenty of nuts; and at last in autumn an

astonishing wealth of different kinds of mushrooms.

The Rajevskis would sometimes make long
excursions in summer when the strawberries
were ripe, and in autumn when the mushroom
season was at hand. These expeditions required
a good deal of preparation ; all had to be ready
on the previous evening. At daybreak two or
three telegas stood before the chief entrance.
There were stir and bustle all over the house,
servants carrying down provisions, a samovar,
china, glasses and empty jars and baskets for
collecting the mushrooms, children running in
everybody's way, dogs barking and nearly upsetting the people.

At last everything is ready : the party, con-
sisting of the governess, the tutor, the three
children and a score of servants, get up into the
carriages, and off they go.

The first halt is to be made at the gamekeeper's house, about seven miles from the
manor. The carriages are jolting slowly along
on the muddy road in the wood. You see nothing but fir-trees all round, high and melancholy
with their dark brown stems; only along the
edges of the road are narrow lines of shrubs,
hazel, elder-bushes ; here and there some red

trembling aspens in their variegated autumn-
tints, or a picturesque mountain-ash with its
brilliant vermilion berries. Suddenly you hear
screams from one of the carriages, the driver's
cap sticks to a dripping wet birch-branch, which
hangs down over the road; when he tries to
catch it somebody shakes the branch, sending a
shower of fragrant dew over all the persons in
the carriage, which calls forth peals of laughter
and jokes.

Now they stop at the gamekeeper's lodge. It
is roofed with planks, and looks cleaner and more
comfortable than most cottages in ' White
Russia.' It stands in a little meadow, and—a
rare luxury for a peasant in this country—is
surrounded by a small garden, where you can see
some red poppies and a few yellow sunflowers in
the midst of the cabbages; some apple-trees, too,
covered with beautiful red apples, the owner's
particular pride, because he has planted them
himself.

The gamekeeper is about seventy, his long
beard is snow-white, but he looks healthy and
strong with his grave dignified face. He is taller
and more robust than most of his countrymen,
and his face reflects the surrounding woods'
majestic calm. All his children are provided

for, his daughters are married, and his sons earn their living as artisans. Now he lives alone with his wife and an adopted child, a boy whom they have taken home to them in their old age.

As soon as his wife catches sight of the visitors she puts the samovar to the fire, and then the old couple meet their guests at the door, bowing deeply, and inviting them to take a cup of tea. The house is neat and clean, but the room is stuffy, and smells unpleasantly of incense and lamp-oil. On account of the winter cold the windows are very small and tightly closed. It is rather hard to breathe here, but the room contains so many interesting things, that the children readily put up with this drawback and begin to look about with curiosity. The clay floor is strewn with fir branches, benches are standing along the walls, and a jackdaw with clipped wings is hopping about without being in the least disturbed by the presence of a black cat, which is sitting on its hind legs washing itself, whilst it looks at the intruders with half-closed eyes and feigned indifference. In one corner stands a large wooden table covered with a white embroidered cloth, and above it hangs a shrine with a Saint and some very old and ugly pictures.

The gamekeeper is said to be a Rascolnik (sectarian), and very likely it is owing to this, circumstance that his home is so clean and comfortable, for it is a well-known fact that the Rascolniks never go to the public-house, and that they keep their homes clean and their lives pure. It is also said that he pays a considerable fee to the Ispravnik (police-officer), and to the priest for not interfering with his religion by forcing him to go to the parish church or by superintending his sectarian worship. He is supposed never to eat anything in the house of an orthodox person, and in his own house he has particular vessels for preparing food for orthodox visitors. Of whatever rank his guests may be, he never offers them anything in a cup or on a dish which he uses himself. The children are very curious to know if 'uncle Jacob,' as they call him, thinks them unclean, but they dare not ask him. They are very fond of uncle Jacob, and it is their greatest delight to visit him. When now and then he comes to Palibino, he always brings them some present, which is more to their taste than all their expensive toys. Once he brought them a young elk, which they kept for a long time in an enclosure of the park, but which never got quite tame.

The large copper samovar stands steaming on the table, and several peculiar dishes are served, sour milk prepared in a very savoury way, and pancakes with poppy-jam, cucumber with honey, delicacies which the children never get anywhere else. The host makes the others eat without partaking of anything himself, and has a serious conversation with the tutor. Though uncle Jacob uses local expressions which the children do not understand, they like to hear him talk, and admire his knowledge of the forest and of all animals, whose lives and habits he seems to know.

It is nearly six o'clock in the morning, and time to start for the day's work. So the party spreads all round in the wood, giving signals now and then to show where they are.

At three o'clock there is a second halt. On the meadow where the horses are grazing the coachman has lit a fire. A servant fetches water from the nearest brook; a cloth is spread on the grass and the meal is got ready. For that day the barrier between master and servant seems broken down, everybody has something to tell, and to show the result of his labour.

After the meal, work is taken up again, but with less zeal than before. Tania, who has been working hard the whole day, has become indifferent to the mushrooms, and is admiring the beautiful scenery. The sun is setting, and its slanting beams throw a golden hue on the naked stems. The little lake seems unnaturally calm, as if spell-bound; its water is almost black, with only one brilliant red spot on its surface.

It is time to think of the home-journey. The party is huddled together in the carriages. During the day, each has been so absorbed in his or her own affairs that nobody has paid much attention to anybody else. But now they all burst out laughing at the sight they present. Faces, hair, and dresses are in wild disorder. The head-gear particularly is most original; one of the girls has just a large bunch of mountain-ash berries in her black tangled hair, another has made herself a helmet of ferns, a third has fixed a large red toad-stool on a stick, holding it up like an umbrella. Tania looks like a little bacchante, with a long branch of wild hops tied round her head, its yellowish green leaves mixing with her brown hair; her cheeks are glowing and her eyes sparkling. Her brother calls her a gipsy queen.

However, the home-drive is very quiet, as everybody feels tired, but Tania lies awake a long time that evening before she can go to sleep.

Opposite to the wood, on the other side of the manor, was the garden, which went down to a lake, beyond which you saw green fields and meadows. Here and there some miserable little villages peeped out among the green surroundings — cottages which looked more like dens of wild beasts than like human dwellings.

The government of Vitebsk is far from being so fertile as the black-earth-belt in Little Russia. The peasants in White Russia are noted for their poverty. The Emperor Nicholas called White Russia a penniless beauty, and the Tamboj government a rich merchant-lady.

In the midst of this wild country, Palibino, with its massive stone walls, its peculiar foreign style of architecture, its terraces bordered with roses, its large hothouses and orangeries, stands out in striking contrast.

Even in summer it is a very calm and lonely place, but in winter the country seems perfectly dead ; all is covered with snow. From the window you see nothing but an endless white plain. For many hours no living creature appears on the road, only at rare intervals a sledge, which is dragged slowly along by a skinny old horse. Sometimes at night the wolves come quite near to the manor. Tania remembers a beautiful winter night; the cold was so intense that it almost stopped your breath. There was no moon, but the snow and millions of large brilliant stars made it quite light. The family was assembled in the large drawing-room; they had had their tea; the children had not yet gone to bed; their mother was playing the piano, and their father smoking and playing patience, when Ilia, the valet, appeared at the door.

'What is the matter?' Ivan Sergejevitsch asked.

'The wolves have gathered near the lake; I thought perhaps your Excellence might like to see them and hear them howl.'

The children got very excited, and were allowed to go out on the terrace with the valet.

First there was deep silence for some moments, but at length a long trembling howl was heard; instantly others answered, and a strange concert began, so sad and gloomy that it made you feel quite melancholy. Even Polka, the dog, felt very uncomfortable, drew in his tail between his legs, and kept close to the children. A nervous shiver seized them all, and they hurried into the warm cosy room again.

VIII

ANIUTA

SHORTLY after the Rajevskis had gone to live in the country, the Polish revolt took place, and its waves were bound to touch Palibino, which lay on the border between Russia and Lithuania Most of the wealthy landowners were Poles. Several of these were more or less compromised; some had their property confiscated, and nearly all were heavily fined. A great number left their homes voluntarily and went abroad. During the first years which succeeded the revolt, there were scarcely any young people in these parts. Only children and old people were left —poor timid creatures who were afraid of their own shadows; besides a few civil officials, merchants, and small proprietors.

Under these circumstances, life in the country could not be cheerful to a young girl like Aniuta, especially as she did not care for any of the pleasures and pastimes which country life can offer. Her whole education had aimed at making her a shining star in society. From her seventh year she used to be the queen of the children's balls in the large towns where her parents lived, while her father was in active service. Ivan Sergejevitsch was proud of his daughter's triumphs; he used to say, 'Wait till Aniuta is presented at Court, she will soon turn the heads of all the Grand Dukes.' Of course, this was only a joke, but unfortunately the children, especially Aniuta herself, took it in real earnest.

Aniuta was a fine girl, tall and shapely, with delicate complexion and fair curly hair; she might almost be called a positive beauty; besides, she had a peculiar charm of manners, and was herself quite aware that she would be able to lead in any society, if she chose. Under these circumstances, she thought it dreadful to waste her time in the dull solitude of Palibino.

Now and then she would go to her father with tears in her eyes, and reproach him for keeping her imprisoned in the country. The first time he answered with a smile and a joke, but when she repeated her complaint, he explained to her that, under the present difficult circumstances, it was the landowner's duty to remain on his property, if he did not want to be ruined. Aniuta could say nothing in reply, she only felt that these reasons did not make life pleasanter to her, and that she was wasting the young years which would never come back again. So she shut herself up and cried bitterly.

Ivan Sergejevitsch used to send his wife and eldest daughter to St Petersburg once a year, during the winter season, to spend a month or six weeks with his sister-in-law; but these visits were expensive, and scarcely of any use. They only increased Aniuta's thirst for pleasures without satisfying it. Serious interests were out of the question in the circle where they moved, and no acceptable 'parti' had presented itself as yet.

These few weeks in the capital went so fast, that Aniuta had scarcely begun thoroughly to enjoy herself when she had to leave town and return to solitude at home, where she spent her time in regretting past pleasures, and in dreaming of future triumphs.

In order to find some occupation for her restless mind, she would take now one hobby, now another, and the other members of the family would generally join her in her projects, as they brought some life and change into the general dulness.

But nobody clung to her with more intense interest and sympathy than Tania, who admired her sister immensely, although her love was mixed with the kind of jealousy one feels secretly, almost unconsciously, of very near and dear relations, whom one wishes to resemble in every way.

Aniuta's first besetting mania was novel-reading, and she was particularly fond of historical novels about the times of chivalry. They were quite a revelation to her, and her lively imagination revelled in this marvellous and romantic world, and applied its ideas to herself and her surroundings. She could easily fancy herself a heroine of romance, and Palibino an old mediæval castle, and she always dated her letters from ' Château Palibino.'

There was a room at the top of a tower which was never used ; Aniuta had it cleansed from the dust and cobwebs of years, the walls covered with ancient tapestry, and decorated with arms from the lumber-room ; and she made it her own private residence. Her slender figure with the tight-fitting white dress, and her long fair hair, were very suitable for a noble damsel of the middle ages. There she would sit in her tower, bending over her frame and embroidering the family coat of arms in beads and gold thread, now and then casting glances down the road looking out for the hero of her dreams.

> 'Sœur Anne, sœur Anne, ne vois-tu rien venir?
> Je ne vois que la terre qui poudroit et l'herbe qui verdoit?'

However, instead of the expected knight, she only sees the Ispravnik and some excise-officers, or an old Jew who comes to buy cattle or whisky at Palibino.

At last, 'soeur Anne' got tired of waiting for her hero, and her romantic fit passed as suddenly as it had begun.

One day a very sentimental book, 'Harold,' by Bulwer Lytton, fell into her hands. The story runs thus :—

After the battle of Hastings, Edith finds the dead body of her lover, King Harold, among those slain on the battle-field. Shortly before his death he had committed perjury, and he died without time for repentance ; so his soul is condemned to eternal punishment.

From that day Edith disappears ; nobody ever

hears from her, she is dead to all. Many years pass, and her name is almost forgotten.

But on a distant shore, amidst mountains and wild forests, is a convent, well known for the severity of its order. Among the nuns is one who has made a vow never to speak, and who is venerated by the whole convent for her charity. She never allows herself any rest ; prayers fill up most of her time when she is not nursing the sick or assisting the needy. Wherever there is a dying person she is found at the bedside imprinting the parting kiss on his forehead with her sealed bloodless lips.

Nobody knows who she is or whence she came. Twenty years ago a woman in a black cloak knocked at the convent gate, and after a long secret interview with the Abbess, she remained there for ever. Now her last hour is at hand. All the nuns gather around her deathbed.

The priest enters. With the power conferred on him by our Lord, he dispenses the dying nun from her vow, and exhorts her to confess who she is, and what is the particular sin that weighs on her mind.

The nun makes an effort to sit up in her bed. The long silence has paralysed her lips, it seems as if she had lost the gift of speech. For a few

R

moments her mouth moves convulsively without producing any audible sound. But obeying her confessor's command, she succeeds at last, though her voice, having been mute for so many years, sounds hollow and unnatural.

'I am Edith,' she says, 'I am the bride of Harold, the slain king.'

On hearing this cursed name the nuns are seized with horror, and make the sign of the cross. But the priest says: 'My daughter, it was a great sinner you loved here on earth. King Harold is condemned by the Church, our holy Mother, and he can never find forgiveness—he is burning for ever in hell. But God has seen your long atonement and taken pity on your tears of repentance. Go in peace! in Paradise you will find another immortal bridegroom.'

A sudden flush appears on Edith's waxen cheeks.

'What is Paradise to me without Harold!' she exclaims. 'If Harold has not found forgiveness, may God never call me to His Paradise!'

The nuns are horror-stricken, but the dying woman makes a superhuman effort; she starts from her couch and falls on her knees in front of the crucifix.

'Almighty God!' she bursts out, 'for some

hours' torments suffered by Thy Son Thou hast taken the burden of sin from humanity. But I have suffered a slow, torturing death for twenty years. Thou knowest my sufferings, Thou hast seen them. If they have gained me Thy mercy, forgive Harold! Give me a token before I die —while we say the Lord's prayer, allow the light in front of the crucifix to kindle of itself, and I shall know that Harold has found salvation.'

The priest says the Lord's prayer slowly and distinctly ; the nuns repeat the words in a low voice. They all feel deep pity for the unhappy Edith, and each of them would gladly sacrifice her own life to save Harold's soul. Edith lies stretched on the floor ; her death-struggle has begun ; the last flickering life is concentrated in her eyes, which stare fixedly on the image of Christ.

The light remains unkindled.

The priest has finished his prayer, and adds his Amen in a melancholy tone.

No miracle ! No forgiveness for Harold !

Edith's lips murmur and curse, and her life is gone.

This book marked a revolution in Aniuta's inner life. For the first time she put the question to herself: 'Is there a future life, or does death put an end to everything? Can two lovers meet in another world and recognise each other?'

With passionate energy she now took up this question, as if she were the first who had ever asked it, and she felt as if she could not live unless she had an answer. And this crisis in Aniuta's mind threw its reflection on her younger sister.

It was a beautiful summer evening at sunset, the air was delightful, and through the open windows came the scent of roses and new-mown hay; from the farm yard one heard distant voices and lowing of cattle—all the sounds that fill the air on a summer evening in the country. Tania was ten years old then, and she felt very happy. She had escaped a few moments from her governess's superintendence, and rushed up to the top of the tower to see what her sister was doing.

And there on the sofa, with floating hair, on which the parting sunbeams are shining, lies Aniuta, crying as if her heart would break.

Tania, frightened to death, cries out: 'But, dearest Aniuta, whatever is the matter?' No answer.

Aniuta kept silent a long while; at last she said: 'You are too young to understand; I don't cry over myself, but over all men. You are a child, you cannot think of such serious matters. I have been a child too, but this terrible, this wonderful book has made me look more deeply into the enigma of life, it has made me see how false and frivolous the things are for which we live. The most glorious happiness, the warmest love—all ends in death. And what awaits us on the other side—if anything awaits us at all—we don't know, we shall never know here! Dreadful! awful!'

She burst into tears again, and buried her head in a cushion.

All this would probably have made a grown-up person smile, but Tania was half dead with terror, awed by the deep thoughts that filled Aniuta's mind. All the beauty of the evening was gone for her, and she felt ashamed to have been so gay.

'But we know there is a God, and we shall go to him after death,' she tried to object.

Aniuta looked into her face with a gentle, forbearing smile, just like an old, experienced person.

'Oh, yes, you have your pure and innocent faith! We won't talk any more about it,' she said, in a melancholy tone, but, at the same time, with such an expression of conscious superiority, that Tania felt ashamed of herself.

The following days Aniuta went about in a sad but gentle mood, looking as if she had resigned all worldly pleasures. What was the use of loving, longing, and hoping for anything, if death put an end to it all?'

Novels were done with now; Aniuta hated them. She took up the 'Imitation of Christ,' and resolved to follow the example of Thomas à Kempis, and to kill her doubts by self-torment and resignation.

She was kind and indulgent to everybody; but it made Tania quite sad to see this expression on her sister's face.

Aniuta's pious mood was respected by those surrounding her; they treated her with gentle consideration, like an invalid or a person who has had a great sorrow. Only the governess shrugged her shoulders incredulously, and her father made a joking remark about her 'air ténébreux,' as he called it. But Aniuta received his joke with calm resignation, and she answered the governess with a politeness that aggravated her more than Aniuta's former impudence. Tania felt miserable to see her sister like that, and no longer enjoyed anything herself; at the same time, she was ashamed at her own want of depth, and secretly envied Aniuta her deep, strong character.

However, this mood did not last long. Elena Paulovna's birthday, the 5th of September, was approaching; it was always celebrated as a great festival. All the neighbours for more than thirty miles round—about a hundred persons—came to Palibino, and some special entertainment used to be given that day—fireworks, tableaux vivants, or theatricals.

Elena Paulovna was very fond of theatricals, and was a very talented actress herself. That year, a small stage had been built at Palibino, with scenery, wings, curtain, etc. In the neighbourhood were some good amateur actors, who were always ready to take part. Elena Paulovna did not think it proper to show too much interest in the matter herself, for she wished people to suppose that it was all got up for the sake of her grown-up daughter. And now it was rather awkward that Aniuta had worked herself up into this saintly mood! So she began by degrees, very carefully, to hint at the forthcoming festival. Aniuta did not yield at once; at first she even showed great contempt for the affair. 'So much trouble! What's the use of it?' But at last she gave way, with the air of one yielding to persuasion.

The difficult thing was to find a suitable play,

amusing, yet not too free, and which did not require too elaborate accessories. At last the choice fell upon ' Les œufs de Perette,' a French vaudeville.

It was the first time Aniuta had acted, and of course she had the most important part. The rehearsals began, and she showed an astonishing talent for acting.

And now, all of a sudden, her fear of death, her struggle between faith and doubt, her anxiety about the uncertain ' Hereafter,' vanished. From morning till night her clear voice was heard throughout the house, singing French couplets.

After Elena Paulovna's birthday, Aniuta resumed her tears, but they were shed for a very different reason now. She wept because her father would not consent to her ardent wish to go to a dramatic training school ; she now felt that it was her vocation in life to become an actress.

IX

A NIHILIST

AT the time Aniuta Rajevski passed through her romantic and ascetic crises, the young generation in Russia was seized by very different aspirations and ideals. However, the Rajevskis lived so far away from the focus of new thought, that it took a long time before the waves of the uproar reached their peaceful home. When this happened at last, Aniuta at once fell a prey to them.

How and when the new spirit made its entry at Palibino would be difficult to say. Before the Rajevskis were aware of it, the fermentation came nearer and nearer, and undermined the pillars of their calm patriarchal existence. The danger did not come from one side only, it seemed to be everywhere.

Between the Sixties and Seventies we may say

that all intelligent circles in Russia were taken up by one great conflict—the family-conflict between the old and the young. Parents and children were at variance, not about property or other practical matters, but exclusively about theories and abstract questions—'their views did not agree.' It was only that, but that 'only' was sufficient to make children desert their homes and parents repudiate their children.

It became an epidemic, especially among young girls, to run away from home. In the immediate vicinity of Palibino, fortunately no such thing had occurred, but it was rumoured now from one place, now from another, that a daughter had run away, either to study abroad or to join the Nihilists in St. Petersburg.

It was said that somewhere in the capital a certain mysterious community existed — the terror of parents and teachers—which was said to admit all young girls who wished to leave their homes. Young people of both sexes were supposed to live there in perfect equality. No servants were allowed; ladies had to scrub the floors and work with their own hands. Of course none of the persons who spread these reports had ever set eyes on the community, and nobody knew where it was, nor how it could possibly exist in the face of the police, and yet scarcely anybody doubted its existence.

By and by the tokens of the time began to appear in the immediate vicinity of Palibino.

The priest of the parish, father Phillip, had a son who had been the joy of his parents by reason of his obedience and blameless behaviour. But he had scarcely ended his studies at the Seminary, with splendid testimonials, when this quiet inoffensive youth suddenly came out a refractory son. He flatly refused to take holy orders, though he needed only to stretch out his hand to get a good living. Even his grace the bishop sent for him and exhorted him not to leave the church, hinting very clearly that it only depended upon himself to become a parish priest in one of the richest counties. It is true, he would have to marry one of the late priest's daughters. This was an old custom, the parish being looked upon as the bride's portion. But not even this attractive bait tempted the young man; he preferred to go to St. Petersburg and enlist as a student at the University, though he would have to live there at his own expense, which was almost tantamount to starving.

Poor father Phillip complained bitterly of his son's folly; he would have put up with it, however, if he had chosen to study law, which would have been the most profitable career from a practical point of view. But instead of this the young man chose natural science, and came home the first time he had holidays full of such mad ideas, that men were descended from monkeys, and that it had been proved by Professor Setchenof that there was no soul, only 'reflex movement,' so that father Phillip was horrified, and had recourse to holy water, with which he sprinkled his son.

In former years, when the young man spent his holidays at home, he never neglected to appear at Palibino on birthdays, and to show his respect to the Rajevskis; at dinner-parties he would take his seat at the bottom of the table, as became his position, and do justice to the fare without mixing in the conversation.

But this summer all was changed. At the first birthday which occurred after his arrival, he was conspicuous by his absence. He made his appearance on another day, and when the footman asked what he wanted, he replied that he had come to pay a visit to the general.

Ivan Sergejevitsh had heard various reports about the young nihilist, and it had not escaped his attention that Alexei Philippovitsch had not

turned up at the birthday dinner, although of
course he pretended not to have noticed such
an unimportant circumstance. Now he felt
annoyed that the young man dared to come and
pay him a visit as if he were his equal,* and he
resolved to give him a lesson. So he ordered
the servant to tell him that 'the General's time
for receiving petitions or business communica-
tions was before one o'clock in the morning.'

The faithful Ilia was quite equal to the
occasion, and delivered the message in the spirit
in which it was given. However, the visitor was
not in the least abashed by this rebuke, and
only said, 'Will you please give your master my
respects, and tell him that from this day I shall
never put my foot inside his house.'

Ilia delivered the message, and we can imagine
the sensation it produced, not only in the
Rajevski family, but in the whole neighbourhood.

But worst of all was Aniuta's behaviour. As
soon as she heard what had happened, she
rushed into her father's room, flushed and
panting with emotion, and exclaimed, 'Why

---

* The Russian clergy forms a caste by itself, and stands on a
rather low social level ; they are generally treated with a certain
contempt.

have you offended Alexei Philippovitsch, father?
It is very bad, it is undignified to treat an honest
man like that!' Ivan Sergejevitsch stared at
his daughter. His consternation was so great,
that he could not at first find words to answer
her impertinence. And Aniuta's courage for-
sook her after the first excitement, so that she
retired hastily to her own room.

After having recovered from his amazement,
and thought the matter well over, Ivan Sergejevitsch came to the conclusion that the best plan
would be not to attach much importance to his
daughter's behaviour, but to make fun of it. So
at dinner he sought an opportunity of telling
a story about a princess who undertook to
make herself the champion of a ploughboy, and
of course both were held up to ridicule. Ivan
Sergejevitsch was a past-master in ridicule, and
the children used to dread his sarcasms. But
this time Aniuta listened calmly and coolly to
her father's story, with a mixed expression of
indignation and defiance. And as a further
protest againt the offence to Alexei Philippovitsch, she began to seek every opportunity
of meeting him.

Stephen, the coachman, astonished his fellow-
servants by telling them that he had seen Miss

Aniuta walking alone with the young man in the wood.

'It was great fun to see them; Miss Aniuta looked down all the time, and didn't say anything, only now and then she would swing her sunshade up and down; he was striding along on his stilt-legs—just like a crane, talking as fast as he could and gesticulating with his arms; then he pulled an old torn book out of his pocket and began to read to her—as if he was giving her a lesson!'

Certainly this youth was very unlike the prince of romance, or the mediæval knight of whom Aniuta had dreamt. His long, unshapely figure, thin neck and pale face, his reddish bristling hair, large coarse hands, and badly trimmed nails—all this could not make him a very seductive hero to a young girl with aristocratic habits and tastes. So it was very unlikely that Aniuta's interest in him could be of a romantic kind; evidently there was something else which attracted her.

And so it was indeed. This young man came direct from St Petersburg, and brought the very newest ideas with him. Besides, he had been fortunate enough to see with his own eyes —at a distance only, it is true—several of the great men to whom all young people at that time looked up with enthusiastic admiration—Tschernyschefsky, Dobroljodof, Sljeptsef. This was quite sufficient to render his own person interesting and attractive. Moreover, through him Aniuta could get several books which otherwise she would never have seen. At Palibino only the most solid and respected periodicals were admitted, *La Revue des deux Mondes*, *The Athenæum*, *The Russian Messenger*. As a great concession to public opinion, Ivan Sergejevitsch had been persuaded to subscribe to the *Epocha*, Dostojevsky's periodical. But now Aniuta had found means to get reading of a very different kind ; periodicals of which every new number was considered the great event of the day. Once even her new friend got her a number of Herzen's prohibited weekly paper, *Kolokol* (The Bell).

It would be unjust to accuse Aniuta of appropriating indiscriminately all the new ideas preached by the nihilist. Many of them revolted her, she thought them much too extreme, and censured them sharply. However, Alexei's conversation, and the reading he brought her, pushed her on and on, and every day she was carried further towards his own views.

As autumn went on the young student fell out so completely with his father, that he was asked to go away, and not to come again next vacation. In the mean time, the seed he had sown in Aniuta's mind kept growing and thriving.

There was a thorough change in her whole appearance; she wore a plain black dress with a white collar, and her hair gathered into a net. Balls and similar entertainments were treated with contempt. In the morning she called in poor children and taught them to read, and when she met a peasant woman on her walks she would stop and talk kindly to her.

The most important change was, that Aniuta, who used to hate anything that looked like serious study, had now a perfect mania for learned books. Instead of squandering her pocket-money on frivolity and useless trinkets, she would send for cases full of books, such as 'The Physiology of Life,' 'The History of Civilisation,' etc.

One day she went to her father, and startled him by the request that he would allow her to go to St. Petersburg to study. Ivan Sergejevitsch at first tried to turn it off with a laugh, as he had done when she had asked him to let her live in town.

S

However, this time she was not to be turned off. Neither jokes nor sarcasms had any effect. She insisted with passionate firmness that though her father might feel obliged to remain on his property, there was no reason why she should be chained to the country, where she could find neither occupation nor pleasure.

At last Ivan Sergejevitsch grew angry and fired up : 'If you don't understand that it is the duty of every decent young girl to remain with her parents till she marries, I am not going to waste my time in arguing with such a silly fool !'

Aniuta saw that it was no use insisting ; but from that moment her relations to her father became very strained, and their mutual resentment grew bitterer every day. They only met at dinner, and then they scarcely spoke to one another, or if they spoke there was a sharp sting in every word.

In fact, there was now a deep division in this family. The governess was a bitter antagonist of the new ideas ; she used to call Aniuta a Nihilist and a Progressist, and these nicknames had a peculiarly sharp accent in her mouth. When her instinct told her that there was something extraordinary going on in Aniuta's mind, she at once suspected her of criminal intentions—of running away from home to marry Alexei Philippovitsch, or to join the ill-famed mysterious community. Therefore she took upon herself to spy out all her steps. And Aniuta, feeling that she was suspected, tried to mystify her still more by her manners and appearance.

Elena Paulovna was the only member of the family who pretended not to notice what was going on ; she always tried to smoothe matters down, and to reconcile everybody.

Tania was thirteen by this time, and, of course, the warlike disposition that had taken hold of the family inevitably exercised a bad effect upon her. The governess now persisted in protecting her pupil from the 'Nihilist,' as if she were pest-smitten, and this constant supervision exasperated Tania. She was aware that Aniuta's mind was filled with new and remarkable interests, and she was dying to know what they were about. Whenever she managed to rush up a moment to her sister's room she found her at her writing-table ; but Aniuta would never tell what she was writing, as she had been scolded more than once by the governess for not only going astray herself but for tempting Tania to do wrong too.' Tania, dear, do go away now,' she would say. 'If Malvina Jakovlevna catches you here, there will be a row again, you know !' And Tania went back to the schoolroom very cross with her governess, because it was her fault that Aniuta would never tell her anything. It became more difficult every day for the poor Englishwoman to get on with her pupil.

From the conversation she overheard, Tania had just gathered some such notions as that it was out of fashion for young people to obey their elders, and this of course weakened her own respect for discipline. Now quarrels with her governess occurred daily, until, at last, after an unusually excited scene, Malvina Jakovlevna declared that she was not going to stay any longer with the Rajevskis.

As this threat had been repeated so often, Tania did not take much notice of it. This time, however, it proved to be serious. The governess on her side had gone too far to retract with honour, and on the other side everybody had become so sick of the constant scenes and quarrels that Tania's parents did not attempt to retain her, hoping that perhaps the house might become quieter when she was gone.

But up to the last moment Tania did not believe that her governess was really going.

X

THE GOVERNESS LEAVES. ANIUTA'S AUTHORSHIP.

THE large old-fashioned box has been standing in the hall from early morning. On the top of it are piled up baskets, bags, and parcels, the indispensable battery of luggage, without which no elderly lady can go on a journey. The carriage is waiting outside, servants are running to and fro, only Ilia, the valet, stands motionless, leaning against the wall; his whole attitude expressing a certain contempt; he does not see the use of making all this fuss for such an unimportant event.

The whole family has gathered in the dining-room. According to old custom Ivan Sergejevitsch asks everybody to sit down; master and mistress occupy the seats of honour, the servants fill up a remote corner, modestly sitting down on the edge of their chairs. There is a few minutes' respectful silence; all feel a little nervous and solemn at this moment of parting.

At last, the General gives the signal for rising; he goes up and makes the sign of the cross before the saint, all follow his example, after which they proceed to the last embraces and parting tears.

Tania kept staring at her governess, towards whom her feelings are undergoing a sudden change; the strong woman looks aged and worn; her eyes, those 'thunderbolts,' as the children used to call them, which never failed to detect the smallest offence, are now red and swollen and full of tears; her lips are quivering with emotion. For the first time in her life Tania pitied her. Malvina clasps her in one long embrace, and kisses her with a tenderness she would never have expected.

'Don't forget me, write soon!' It is a very sad thing to part from a child for whom you have lived so many years!' she sobs.

And Tania clings to her and bursts out crying; her heart aches, and she feels as if the loss of her governess were quite irreparable, and as if it foreboded general dissolution. And then her conscience smites her, she is ashamed of her own feelings that very morning, when she was happy

to think that she would be relieved of her governess's yoke. 'It serves me quite right, now she
is going to leave me alone, I am *so* sorry; I would
give ever so much to make her stay,' she says to
herself, and cannot tear herself away.

At last the governess gets into the carriage,
and Tania hurries up stairs to the corner-room,
from whence she has a view down the long
avenue of birches, which leads from the manor
to the high-road. She presses her face against
the window, and her eyes follow the carriage till
it is out of sight. The feeling of her own
guilt hurts her. 'She loved me, she would have
stayed if she had known that I was fond of her
too. Nobody cares for me now, nobody!' she
thinks, and her tears begin streaming afresh.

'Are you crying for Malvina?' her brother asks,
as he runs past her, and looks surprised and in-
credulous. 'Leave her alone, Fedia, she is quite
right,' she hears one of her aunts say; it is her
father's sister, whom none of the children like,
because they think she is false. Tania does not
care to be comforted by her, and impatiently
shaking off the hand with which her aunt is
gently patting her shoulder, she rushes to the
school-room, but seeing it empty she bursts into
a fresh fit of tears. At last she finds a little

comfort in thinking that nobody now will prevent her from being with her sister as much as she pleases, and off she rushes to see what Aniuta is doing.

She finds her pacing up and down the large hall, lost in her own thoughts, which are evidently of a very exciting nature. Tania knows from experience how difficult it is to get hold of her attention at such moments, but after having waited a while she gets impatient and tries to rouse her.

'Aniuta, I feel *so* sad, lend me one of your books to read,' she says in a pleading voice. No answer. 'Aniuta, what are you thinking of?' Tania says at last. 'Now do stop a moment, there's a dear!'

'You are much too young to hear about such things,' is the contemptuous reply.

But this was a little too bad, and Tania gets angry at last. 'How unkind you are! you won't even speak to me! Now Malvina is gone, I thought we should be such good friends. But if you drive me away, I shall go, and I shall *never*, *never* love you again!'

And Tania runs away swallowing her tears,—but suddenly her sister calls her back. In her own heart Aniuta is dying to pour out all that fills her mind, and as there is nobody else she can speak to she contents herself with Tania.

'Look here,' she says, 'if you promise to be silent as the grave about it, I will tell you a great secret.'

Tania's tears stop immediately, her resentment vanishes instantly; of course she vows silence, and is very curious to know what her sister is going to tell her.

'Come to my room!' Aniuta says solemnly, 'I will show you something—something you will never guess.'

And she takes Tania to her room, and to the old writing-table, where she keeps her important papers. Slowly and carefully she pulls out one of the drawers and takes out a large business-like envelope, with a red seal and stamped *Epocha;* it is addressed to Miss Nikitischna Kusynin (the housekeeper, who adored Aniuta, and would have done anything for her), but out of the large envelope Aniuta takes a smaller one addressed, 'Miss Anna Ivanovna Rajevski,' and holds out a letter to Tania, written in a bold firm hand. It runs as follows :—

'MOST HONOURED MISS ANNA IVANOVNA —Your most kind and confidential letter filled me with such interest that I read your story immediately.

'I confess I began it with a secret misgiving; we editors often have the sad duty of crushing the illusions of young beginners who submit their first literary attempts to our judgment, and in your case this duty would have appeared particularly painful to me. But as I went on, my fear vanished, and I was thoroughly captivated by the youthful freshness and the warm, sincere feeling that breathes throughout your story. These qualities influenced me so much in your favour, that I fear I am too much under the spell as yet to enable me to give you an impartial, categorical answer to your question, "if you are likely to become a great authoress."

'For the present, all I can say is, that I shall be very much pleased to publish your story in the next number of my periodical. In reply to your question, I can only say, write and work— time must do the rest.

'I cannot deny that your story is too naïve in certain respects, that it wants finish, and that there are — forgive my sincerity — faults of grammar. But these defects are of small consequence, and you will get over them if you

persevere in working. The general impression
is decidedly favourable.

'Therefore, I repeat, write, write! I should
be much interested if you could find an opportunity of telling me something about yourself, your age and your surroundings. All this
would help me greatly to judge of your gifts.—
Yours very sincerely,

'DOSTOJEVSKY.'

Tania was dumfounded, the characters danced
before her eyes. The name of Dostojevsky was
well known to her ; it had often been mentioned
in her discussions with her father. She knew that
he was one of the most prominent Russian
authors, but how *could* it be that *he* should write
to Aniuta? What did it all mean? For a
moment the thought flashed through her mind
that Aniuta was joking. She stared at her in
mute surprise, and Aniuta enjoyed it thoroughly.

'Do you see, do you see?' she exclaimed at
last, and her voice trembled with joyful emotion,
'I have written a story and sent it to Dostojevsky, without breathing a word to a single soul
about it. And you see he approves of it, and
accepts it for his paper. So my secret dream is
fulfilled—I am an authoress!"

Tania found no words to express her delight
and surprise; the two sisters were clasped in a
fond embrace, they smiled with tears in their
eyes, and whispered all kind of follies to one
another.

Of course it was out of the question to tell
anybody else of Aniuta's success; her mother
would be terribly frightened, and reveal all to
her husband, and in his eyes the step Aniuta
had taken would be a downright crime. Poor
Ivan Sergejevitsch, he had an aversion for lady
authors, and almost thought them capable of
excesses that had nothing whatever to do with
literature. It was, indeed, the very irony of fate
that he should be the father of an authoress!

He had only known one 'blue-stocking,' he
said, the Countess Rostoptschin (a great poetess).
He had met her in Moscow at the time when she
was a brilliant and celebrated beauty, and had
all the young noblemen at her feet, himself
amongst the number. Many years later he saw
her again abroad, in Baden-Baden, at the green
table. 'I could not believe my eyes,' Ivan Sergejevitsch used to say when he told this story,
'when I saw the countess come in, followed by
a host of vagabonds, all talking and joking in
the most familiar way. She went up to the

gambling table, and staked one sovereign after
another, her eyes sparkling, her face flushed, and
her hair in disorder.   After having lost her last
coin, she turned round, and exclaimed to her
followers : " Eh bien, messieurs, je suis vidée !
Rien ne va plus !—Come, let us drown our grief
in champagne."

' There, you see what becomes of ladies who
take up pen and ink ! '

So, naturally, Aniuta was not impatient to
tell her father of her literary success.   But the
mystery of it lent a peculiar charm to her début
in her new career, and we can imagine the
delight of the two sisters when, some weeks
later, the *Epocha* published the story, 'The Dream,'
by Zuri Orbjolof (the pseudonym Aniuta had
chosen).

The heroine of the story is a young girl like
herself, educated under similar circumstances and
surroundings ; the hero, a young student of the
modern type, whom she meets one evening, and
who leaves a deep impression on her mind.
However, prejudice and conventionality prevent
her from betraying her feelings.   The young man
goes away.   Some time after he appears to her
in a dream, holding out before her beautiful
images of a happy future, in which she sees her-

self leading an active life at his side. Then he
disappears, with these words: 'All this you have
lost!' She awakes and makes up her mind to
go and seek her friend. After many adventures,
and much trouble, she finds the house where he
used to live, but here she is told by a friend of
his that he has died a few days ago of typhoid
fever. She also hears that, in his delirium, he
has sometimes raved about a young girl.

Lilienka (the young girl) returns home, but
nobody ever knows where she has been. She
feels certain that she has thrown away her happiness through her own fault, and dies of grief
shortly after.

Aniuta's first success encouraged her to go on,
and she immediately began a new story and
finished it in a few weeks. Dostojevsky was
much more pleased with this second attempt
than with the first; he thought it riper.

But its course did not run so smooth. The
letter from Dostojevsky fell into the hands of
Ivan Sergejevitsch, and now the storm broke
out!

This happened on the 5th of September, a
memorable day in the annals of the Rajevski
family. It was Elena Paulovna's birthday, and
a large circle of friends were assembled. It

happened to be the day when the weekly post
came to Palibino. The housekeeper, under
whose name Aniuta carried on her correspondence, used to go out and meet the postman and
take out the letters addressed to her before the
bag was taken to the General. But on this day
she was busy on account of the party, and the
man who generally fetched the post had been
celebrating his mistress's birthday by getting
dead drunk, so that a boy had had to be sent in
his stead, and he did not know anything of the
arrangement with regard to the secret correspondence. In this way the letter fell into the
General's hands without any previous examination.

The first thing that caught Ivan Sergejevitsch's
eye was a registered letter addressed to the
housekeeper, and bearing the stamp of the
Epocha. What could it mean? He sent for
the housekeeper and ordered her to open the
letter in his presence.

You can imagine—no, it would be impossible
to imagine the scene that ensued. And worst
of all!—in this letter Dostojevsky happened to
send the payment for the two stories—about 300
rubles. The fact that his daughter received
money from an unknown gentleman appeared

to the General so shameful and offensive that he
had a severe attack of illness.   He suffered from
heart-disease and from gallstone, and the doctors
had declared that strong emotions were dangerous and might be fatal to him.   The whole
family therefore dreaded such a catastrophe.
Now, what would be the effect of this awful
shock? and in presence of all the guests, whose
number had been increased on this occasion by
all the officers from the nearest garrison, who
had brought the military band with them.

Dinner was over long ago, and the young
people were preparing for the dance.   Aniuta
was all smiles and amiability; she knew she
would be the queen of the ball, and was enjoying
her triumphs in anticipation.

They were only waiting for the General's appearance to begin.

Suddenly a servant hurries up to Elena
Paulovna, telling her that his Excellency is
unwell and wants her to come to his study.

There is a general suspense.   Elena Paulovna
disappears, the musicians who are ready to
begin playing are ordered to wait.

Half an hour passes, the guests are becoming
uneasy.   At last Elena Paulovna comes back,
flushed with emotion, but trying to smile and

control herself, and answering all anxious questions by saying that Ivan Sergejevitsch is a little
unwell, and asks to be excused; he hopes they
will begin dancing all the same.

And the ball commences.

Aniuta casts frightened glances at her mother,
and reads in her eyes that something dreadful
has happened. During a momentary interval
she takes her into a corner beseeching her to tell
what is the matter.

'What *have* you done? All is discovered, your
father has read Dostojevsky's letter, and he is
dying of shame and rage.' And poor Elena
Paulovna tries in vain to keep back her tears.

Aniuta is pale as death, and her mother adds
hurriedly, 'For heaven's sake, control yourself!
remember our guests! What a delight it would
be to them to get such food for gossip! Go on—
as if nothing had happened.'

And mother and daughter continue dancing
the whole night, both nearly fainting with fright
in thinking of the storm that awaits them as
soon as the visitors are gone.

And terrible it was indeed!

Ivan Sergejevitsch had locked himself up in
his room, and nobody was admitted. During
the pauses Elena Paulovna and Aniuta had

T

been at his door to listen, and had come back to the party in awful suspense, thinking that he might be ill.

When the house was quiet, at last, he called Aniuta, and the outburst of his anger was dreadful.

Amongst all he said, there was one sentence which imprinted itself for ever in her memory: ' Anything may be expected of a young girl capable of entering into correspondence with an unknown man, and of taking money from him without her parents' knowledge! *Now* you sell your work, but I am not sure that some day you will not sell yourself!'

Poor Aniuta shrank from these awful words. She felt indeed that they were not meant in earnest, but her father spoke with such conviction, his expression was so angry, and at the same time so sad, his authority still so great in her eyes, that for a moment she was seized with a painful doubt. Had she deceived herself? Had she, without knowing it, done something which was dreadfully indecorous?

As usual, after such domestic scenes, everybody looked crestfallen. The servants soon knew all about it. Ilia had been eaves-dropping, as was his praiseworthy habit; he had over-

heard the whole conversation between Ivan Sergejevitsch and Aniuta, and explained it in his
own way.

And, of course, the interesting news spread all
over the neighbourhood, in very exaggerated
proportions, and was the general gossip for a
long time.

By degrees, however, the storm abated. In
the Rajevski family a phenomenon was noticed,
which is not unfrequent in Russian families—the
children educated their parents, beginning with
their mother.

In all scenes between the General and his
children, Elena Paulovna, at first, went entirely
with her husband. His attacks of illness
frightened her, and she was very much displeased
with Aniuta for causing him this grief. Now
and then she would go to her daughter and say
in her most persuasive tone, ' Aniuta dear, now
do give in to your father ; promise that you will
never write again ; you might try to find some
other occupation. When I was young I once
wished to learn the violin, but my father would
not allow it, as he thought it an ungraceful
thing for a lady to do. Well, what was to be
done ? Of course, I did not insist, but took
singing lessons instead. Why, now, can't you

give up that horrid literature, and do something else ? '

However, when she saw that her attempts were useless, and that Aniuta persisted in going about with her melancholy, injured expression, she began to pity her. And then, she could not help being curious to read Aniuta's stories, and feeling a little proud to think that her daughter was an authoress.

So, by degrees, she went over to Aniuta's side, and Ivan Sergejevitsch at last found himself standing quite alone.

In the anger of the first moment he had requested Aniuta to vow that she would never write again, and made his forgiveness depend upon this condition. Aniuta, of course, could not give such a promise ; consequently father and daughter did not speak to one another for several days, and Aniuta did not even appear at dinner. Elena Paulovna continued her mediation.

At last Ivan Sergejevitsch yielded, in so far that he consented to hear Aniuta's story.

And in presence of the assembled family this reading took place. Aniuta, fully conscious of the importance of this moment, read in a voice that trembled with emotion.

The heroine's fate was so like the authoress's that everybody was struck by it. Ivan Sergejevitsch listened in perfect silence. But when Aniuta came to the last page, where Lilienka is dying, and bewails her lost youth, her voice trembled with suppressed sobs, and her father's eyes filled with tears. He rose without saying a word, and left the room. He never spoke to Aniuta about her story, but he treated her with great tenderness, and everybody understood that her cause was gained.

A spirit of gentleness and conciliation seemed to dawn on the family from that day. Its first important token was, that the housekeeper, whom Ivan Sergejevitsch had dismissed in his first wrath, was graciously allowed to remain at her post.

And the next act of forbearance was even more astonishing. Ivan Sergejevitsch permitted Aniuta to write to Dostojevsky, only with the restriction that she was to show him the letter. More still, he promised that, during their approaching visit to St Petersburg, she was to make his personal acquaintance.

When his wife and daughter went to the capital, the General used to remain in the country, as well as Tania, who was under the

superintendence of her governess.   But as Malvina Jakovlevna had left, and her Swiss successor
had not had time to gain perfect confidence,
Elena Paulovna, to Tania's great delight, made
up her mind to take the child with her.

This journey generally took place in January,
when there was excellent sleighing.   They had
to travel about forty miles in a telega, and
twenty-four hours by railway, and great preparations were made in the kitchen for this journey.

And what a wonderful journey it was—through
endless, dense forests, only varied by a number
of lakes, which in winter looked like vast plains
of snow.   To Tania it remains as one of the
brightest memories of her childhood.

XI

A WINTER IN ST. PETERSBURG.
DOSTOJEVSKY

IMMEDIATELY after their arrival in St. Petersburg, Aniuta sent an invitation to Dostojevsky, and the two sisters looked forward to his visit in feverish excitement. However, it turned out to be a great disappointment.

Ivan Sergejevitsch had strongly recommended his wife to be present at their meeting. So, when Dostojevsky arrived at the appointed time, he found Aniuta surrounded by her mother and some old aunts, who were curious to see the celebrated man. Tania had also begged permission to be present. Aniuta was much annoyed, and scarcely opened her mouth. Dostojevsky was disappointed, too, and all Elena Paulovna's attempts to keep up an interesting conversation fell to the ground. Everybody felt uncomfortable, and after having stayed for about half-an-hour, the visitor rose, made a stiff bow to all the ladies, and left without shaking hands with anybody.

Aniuta was very disappointed at having her pleasure spoilt in this way, and her mother felt miserable and guilty, though she scarcely knew why.

Dostojevsky's appearance and manners had left an unfavourable impression. Though a man of little more than forty, he looked rather old and worn; he kept pulling his thin yellow beard and biting his lips, and his conversation was anything but amiable.

However, some days after, he repeated his visit, and this time was fortunate enough to find the two sisters alone. He seized Aniuta's hands, and they sat down on the sofa, and talked together like old friends. Tania sat by in silence, her eyes riveted on Fedor Michajlovitsch, and drinking in every word he said with intense interest. How changed he was this time! He looked so young, was so simple, amiable, and natural in his manners, and so fascinating. Tania was quite taken with him.

'What a sweet little sister you have got!' he said, quite unexpectedly, to Aniuta, and now Aniuta got quite warm in praise of her sister;

she even told him that Tania wrote verses, and
showed him her poems. Dostojevsky read some
of them out loud, and said some kind things
about them. Tania beamed and flushed with
delight; she thought she could have laid down
her life for these two, who were so kind to her,
and whom she admired so much.

They all forgot the time, and three hours had
gone when Elena Paulovna at last came home
from her shopping. She was very much surprised, and a little shocked, when she found
Dostojevsky in the drawing-room alone with
her daughters. However, they all looked so
bright and happy that she soon forgot her
anxiety, and even invited Dostojevsky to stay
and dine with them. From that day he became
a frequent guest in their house. He never
showed to advantage in society, but when alone
with a few intimate friends who understood and
admired him, he was fond of talking, and would
give most interesting and graphic descriptions of
many stirring events of his past life, or he would
tell the contents of some novel he was going to
write.

Some of his brightest recollections were connected with the publication of his first great
novel, ' Poor People; ' it had an immense success,

and was written when he was quite young ; he had sent it to a periodical, 'The Contemporary,' which was published by the famous critic Bolinsky, and received contributions from the rising star the poet Nekrasof, and the celebrated novelist Gregorovitsch. A great and general revival took place at that time in Russian literature. Turgenef, Gontscharof, and Herzen appeared with their first works. The public showed an unusual interest in literary productions, and never had the demand for books and periodicals been so great.

It was the year of revolt, 1848. All Europe was in a state of excitement.

In St. Petersburg, particularly amongst the students at the University and the pupils at the Polytechnicon, numerous small societies were formed, which at first only occupied themselves with literary pursuits. But, as the police had orders to prohibit all societies, of whatever description they might be, the young men were obliged to hold their meetings in secret, and so by degrees they took a political character. It was Petroschevski, an unusually clever man and warm adherent of Fourier, who first conceived the idea of joining all these small societies into one large secret political confederation. However, Petro-

schevski and his party did not aim at open revolt,
nor at any attempt against the Emperor's life,
and their objects appear rather innocent compared
with the Nihilistic propaganda of later years.
The questions discussed at their secret meetings
were mostly of an abstract character, and occasionally rather naïf, as for instance : Can we
reconcile the killing of spies and traitors with the
principles of philanthropy? or, Are the doctrines
of the Greek Church incompatible with Fourier's
ideals?

Dostojevsky joined Petroschevski's party. It
appeared from subsequent investigations that his
crime had been to read an account of Fourier's
principles at one of the secret meetings, and to
have been involved in a plan for establishing a
secret printing office.

The punishment for this offence was—Siberia! *

April 23rd, 1849, was a fatal day to the Pet-
roschevskists ; the chief and thirty of his adher-
ents were arrested on that day.

Dostojevsky gave a detailed and graphic
account of their long imprisonment and trial.
' It was not till February 23rd, the following

---

* It must be remembered that Dostojevsky was an officer in the
Russian army.—(*Translator's note*).

year, that my sentence was read to me in my
cell.   I was condemned to be shot !

'Nothing was said about the time, but scarcely
an hour had passed, when the gaoler appeared
and told me to put on my own clothes.   Under
strong escort I was led out into the yard, where
nineteen of my companions were waiting.   It
was seven o'clock in the morning.   We were put
into carriages, four in each, accompanied by a
soldier.

' "Where are we going?" we asked ; "I must
not tell you," the soldier replied.   And as the
carriage windows were covered with ice we could
see nothing outside.

'At last we reached Senajenovski Square.   In
the middle of it a scaffold was raised, up to
which we were led and ranged in two lines.   We
were so carefully watched that it was impossible
to say more than a few words to those that stood
nearest.

'A sheriff appeared on the scaffold and read
out our sentence of death ; it was to be executed
instantly.

'Twenty times the fatal words were repeated :
" Sentenced to be shot ! "   And so indelibly were
the words graven into my memory, that for years
afterwards I would awake in the middle of the

night, fancying I heard them being read.   But at
the same time I distinctly remember another circumstance: the officer, after having finished the
reading, folded the paper and put it into his
pocket, after which he descended from the scaffold.   At this moment the sun broke through the
clouds, and I thought, "It is impossible, they can't
mean to kill us!" and I whispered these words to
my nearest companion, but instead of answering,
he only pointed to a line of coffins that stood
near the scaffold, covered with a large cloth.

'All my hope vanished in an instant, and I
expected to be shot in a few minutes.

'It gave me a great fright, but I determined
not to show any fear, and I kept talking to my
companion about different things.   He told me
afterwards that I had not even been very pale.

'All of a sudden a priest ascends the scaffold,
and asks if any of the condemned wishes to confess his sins.   Only one accepted the invitation,
but when the priest held out the crucifix we all
touched it with our lips.

'Petroschevsky and two others, who were considered the most culpable, were already tied to
the poles and had their heads covered with a
kind of bag, and the soldiers stood ready to fire
at the command " Fire!"

'I thought I might perhaps have five minutes more to live, and awful these moments were. I kept staring at a church with a gilt dome, which reflected the sunbeams, and I suddenly felt as if these beams came from the region where I was to be myself in a few moments!

'Then there was a general stir. I was too short-sighted to discern anything, but I felt that something extraordinary was happening. At last I descried an officer, who came galloping across the square, waving a white handkerchief. He was sent by the emperor to announce our pardon. Afterwards we learned that the sentence of death had only been a threat, intended as "a lesson not to be forgotten." But this lesson had fatal consequences for many of us. When Grigorief was released from the pole, he had become mad through the terror he had undergone whilst waiting for the fatal shot, and he never recovered his reason. Nor do I think that any of us escaped without lifelong injury to his nervous system.

'Besides, when we were taken up to the scaffold, they took off our clothes, so that we had spent more than twenty minutes standing in our bare shirts in a cold of 22 deg. Réaumur below freezing point! When we came back to our prisons, some of us had their ears and toes frozen; one got inflammation of the lungs, which ended in consumption. As for myself, I don't remember to have had the slightest sensation of the cold.

'Our sentence of death had been changed to eight years' penal servitude in Siberia, and many years' subsequent exile.'

Aniuta and Tania knew that Dostojevsky suffered from epileptic fits, but to them this disease was connected with a kind of mysterious horror, so they never dared breathe a word about it. To their great surprise one day he broached the subject himself, and told them under what circumstances the first fit had seized him.

He had left his prison and was living as a colonist somewhere in Siberia. He suffered dreadfully from solitude at the time, and sometimes several months would pass without his seeing a living creature. One day—it was Easter-eve—one of his old friends came on an unexpected visit. But in the delight of their meeting they forgot the holy festival, and sat up all night in endless talk about literature and philosophy, and at last about religion. His visitor was an atheist, Dostojevsky himself a believer, and each was thoroughly convinced that he was right.

'There *is* a God, there *is*!' Dostojevsky exclaimed at last, beside himself with enthusiasm.

And at that moment the church bells chimed for morning service. The air vibrated with these solemn tones. 'And I felt,' Dostojevsky continued, 'how heaven descended on earth, and carried me away. " There *is* a God," I exclaimed, and then I lost consciousness.'

' Healthy persons like yourself,' he said, 'have no idea of the bliss we feel the moment before the seizure. Mahomet says in his Koran that he has been in Paradise. The ignorant and undiscerning call him a liar and an impostor. No ! he does not lie ! He had really been in Paradise during an attack of epilepsy, from which he suffered like myself.

' I cannot tell if this bliss lasts for seconds, hours, or months, but, believe me, I would not exchange it for all the happiness life can give !'

Dostojevsky said these last words in a peculiar whisper. The sisters felt spellbound by the magnetic power of his words. Suddenly the same thought struck them : he is going to have a fit now !

There was a twitch in his face and a contraction about his mouth.

Dostojevsky read their thoughts, and suddenly stopped with a smile. 'Don't be afraid,' he said, 'I always know beforehand when the fit is coming on.'

The young girls felt rather embarrassed and ashamed that he had guessed their thoughts, and did not know what to answer. Soon·after Dostojevski left, but he told them afterwards that he had had a fit the following night.

Elena Paulovna and Dostojevsky had become great friends, and she even persuaded him to accept an invitation to a large farewell party she was going to give before leaving town.

Unfortunately, this entertainment turned out a complete failure, and Dostojevsky's presence was a fatal mistake. He felt more uncomfortable than ever in this large heterogeneous society. As usual on similar occasions, he was rude and unpleasant. He tried to monopolise Aniuta the whole evening, and took great offence when Elena Paulovna called her daughter away to attend to her other guests. The fact was that Dostojevsky was seriously in love, and that one of the gentlemen present, a young officer, had roused his jealousy by the marked attentions he paid the

U

young girl. Some very unpleasant scenes occurred in the course of the evening, and Dostojevsky scandalised the party by a wild outburst of temper, in which he threw out a broad hint about parents selling their daughters for worldly advantages.

After this party the relations between Dostojevsky and Aniuta were quite changed. He was irritable and exacting, and tormented her with his jealousy ; she no longer looked up to him as before, but seemed to find pleasure in teasing him.

In the early stage of their acquaintance Aniuta had gladly given up all other pleasures on the days when Dostojevsky was expected, and when he was in the room her thoughts had been entirely taken up with him. Now all this had changed. When he came whilst other visitors were present, she quietly continued entertaining them, and if she received an invitation for the days when Dostojevsky had promised to come, she wrote to him excusing herself.

Then he used to appear the following day, and to be very excited. Aniuta, pretending not to notice his bad humour, would take up some work.

This irritated him still more ; he would sit in a corner without saying a word.

'Where did you go yesterday?' he would burst out at last in an irritated tone.

'To a ball,' Aniuta replies.

'You danced?'

'Of course.'

'With your cousin?'

'With him and with others.'

'And you find pleasure in those things!'

Aniuta shrugs her shoulders.

'Why shouldn't I?' she replies, resuming her work.

'You are a frivolous, thoughtless doll,' he exclaims at last.

In this way they used to talk.

But in proportion as the relations between these two seemed to become more strained, the friendship between Dostojevsky and Tania grew warmer. Of course her blind admiration flattered him, and he would frequently hold up Tania as an example to her sister.

When Aniuta pretended not to understand his paradoxes, Fedor Michajlovitsch would fire up, exclaiming:

'You have a shallow and narrow mind! look at your sister! She understands me, she has depth and delicacy of mind.'

On these occasions Tania blushed with delight,

and she would have cut herself in pieces to prove how well she understood him.

And indeed, strange as it may seem, Tania did understand Dostojevsky. She guessed his warm and tender feelings, she honoured him, not only on account of his genius, but because of his sufferings. His originality captivated her and fertilized her own imagination.

If Dostojevsky had been able to look into this young heart, he would have been deeply touched to see the place he occupied in it.

In the depths of her heart Tania was very much pleased that Dostojevsky appeared less infatuated with Aniuta than he had been at first, and yet she was ashamed of this feeling, as if it were a kind of treason.

Fedor Michajlovitsch called Tania his little friend, and he would even commend her outward appearance at the expense of her sister.

'You think you are good-looking,' he would say; 'I can assure you, your sister will be much prettier than you some day. Her face is much more expressive, and then she has a pair of genuine gipsy-eyes! You — why, you have a rather pleasant little German face, that's all.'

Aniuta smiled contemptuously; but Tania

swallowed eagerly the unusual praise of her beauty.

She would have liked to know what her sister thought of all this, and if she herself would indeed become good-looking some day. So when they were going to bed that evening she said, 'What funny things Fedor Michajlovitsch was saying to-day!'—trying to look as unconcerned as possible.

'What do you mean?' Aniuta asked; she had evidently forgotten the whole conversation.

'Oh well, that about the gipsy-eyes, and about my being good-looking,' says Tania, blushing deeply.

Aniuta turns her graceful neck and looks at Tania with a sly, expressive glance.

'So you fancy Fedor Michajlovitsch thinks you good-looking, better looking than me?' she asks.

The wonderful mysterious smile in Aniuta's green eyes, and her fair flowing curls, make her look like a mermaid. In the large looking-glass opposite the bed, Tania sees her own little dark person beside that of her sister. It would be a great mistake to say that she feels satisfied with the comparison, but her sister's cold self-complacent tone irritates her, and she says with some temper—

'Oh, well, tastes differ!'

'Indeed, tastes are queer sometimes,' Aniuta says calmly, and continues to brush her hair.

They put out the light, but Tania keeps on brooding over the same thing.

'Is it possible?' she asks herself, 'Can Fedor Michajlovitsch really think me better looking than Aniuta?' and she adds these words to her prayer,

'Good Lord, let all the world admire Aniuta, but let Fedor Michajlovitsch only think that I am prettier.'

But a bitter disappointment was in store for poor Tania.

Dostojevsky had strongly advised Tania to keep up her music. She was not very musical, but her regular daily practising had given her some execution, a good touch and facility in reading. She once happened to play a piece to Dostojevsky—variations on Russian ballads— which pleased him particularly, because he was in a mood to enjoy music, and so he became quite enthusiastic about it and broke out in exaggerated praise of Tania's musical gifts. Of course this was sufficient for Tania to make a fresh start. She took lessons of a first-rate teacher, and spent every leisure hour at the

piano. She was going to prepare a great surprise for Dostojevsky in practising the 'Sonate
pathétique,' which he had said was his favourite
piece.

It was rather a difficult task, but after some
time Tania mastered it pretty well, and was
only awaiting an opportunity to exhibit her
skill.

One day shortly before the Rajevskis were to
leave town, the two sisters were alone, as their
mother and aunts were going out to dinner.
Dostojevsky came in the evening; he seemed a
little nervous and queer, but not irritable, as he
was wont to be of late.

Tania, thinking how delighted he would be to
hear his favourite piece of music, sat down and
began to play. Anxious to do her very best,
she was soon so entirely absorbed by her music,
that she forgot everything else. At last she
had done, and feeling that she had really done
well was waiting for the applause from him for
whom all this trouble had been taken. But there
was deep silence. Tania looked round—the
room was empty.

Her heart sank; a vague misgiving seized her.
She went into the next room—nobody was there.
At last she came to the little corner-room, and

lifted the curtain which separated it from the other apartments; — and what did she see? Aniuta and Dostojevsky sitting together on the sofa! the room was dimly lighted, and Aniuta's face was hidden by the lamp-shade, but Dostojevsky's face was seen distinctly—it was pale and excited; he was holding Aniuta's hand, and bending towards her; he spoke in a passionate whisper.

'Anna Ivanovna, don't you understand that I have loved you from the first moment I saw you; nay, before I saw you, when I read your letters? I love you, not as a friend—no, passionately, with all my heart—'

And Tania! She nearly fainted. A bitter feeling of loneliness came over her; she felt deeply wronged; all the blood rushed to her heart and then to her head.

She dropped the curtain and rushed out of the room, upsetting a chair in her hurry.

Her sister started. 'Is it you, Tania?' she said. But Tania neither answered nor stopped till she reached her own room at the other end of the house. She tore off her dress, fell on her bed and buried her face in the pillows.

Her heart was overflowing. Till now she had never fully realised her feeling for Dostojevsky,

not in the deepest recesses of her heart had she
owned to herself that she was in love with him,
and indescribable were the feelings of bitterness,
wrong and shame that swelled her poor heart in
this terrible hour.

At last she began to wish that her sister would
come.

'They don't care for me, they wouldn't care if
I were dying! Oh, I wish I could die now!'
and her grief found vent in a flood of tears.

Sleep was out of the question. At last Tania
hears the door-bell ring and quick steps outside;
the ladies were coming home, she heard them
talking, and distinguished Dostojevsky's voice
taking leave. The hall door was shut, and Aniuta's
steps approached in the passage.

Tania could not bear the light that fell on her
face, neither could she endure to meet Aniuta's
happiness, so she turned round pretending to be
asleep.

Aniuta went up to her : 'You're not asleep?'
she said. No answer.

'Well, if you are offended, I can't help it—it's
all the worse for you, you won't hear anything!'
Aniuta said, and went to bed as if nothing had
happened.

The next day Tania felt miserable, and went

in feverish expectation of what Aniuta would have to tell her. She put no questions, but there was a hostile feeling in her heart towards her sister, and when Aniuta came up and tried to caress her, Tania pushed her away vehemently in a flash of anger. This offended Aniuta again, and she left Tania to her own sad humour.

Tania dreaded the moment when Dostojevsky should come, and expected him every minute, but he never came. They sat down to dinner—no Dostojevsky.

There was a concert in the evening. 'Of course Aniuta will stay at home, *he* will come, and they will be alone!' Her heart ached with jealousy. No! Aniuta went to the concert with them, and was in high spirits all the time.

When the two sisters were going to bed that night, Tania could not control herself any longer. Without looking at her sister, she said :

'When do you expect Fedor Michajlovitsch?'

Aniuta smiled. 'Well, you don't want to know anything, you won't talk to me, you are offended!'

Her voice was so kind and gentle that Tania melted immediately, and her love for Aniuta came back.

She crept up into her sister's bed, clung to her, and burst out crying. Aniuta patted her head.

'You little fool,' she said, 'silly little thing!'
she repeated tenderly. At last she could not help
bursting out into loud laughter:

'Oh, I never heard such a thing before! You
go and fall in love with a man three times as old
as yourself!'

These words, this laughter, awakened a mad
hope in Tania.

'Then you don't love him?' she asked, whispering in breathless emotion.

Aniuta kept thinking for some moments.

'You see,' she began, evidently somewhat
embarrassed, 'of course, I like him very much,
and admire him exceedingly. He is as clever
as original, such a genius! But—how shall I
explain—I don't really love him in such a way;
I mean not so that I should like to marry him!'
she burst out at last.

What a load fell from Tania's heart! How
bright she felt at once! She clasped her sister's
neck and kissed her fondly. Aniuta continued
talking.

'Do you know I am quite surprised myself
that I don't love him. He is *so* good, *so* amiable!
At first I really thought I should care for him.
But *I* am not the kind of wife *he* wants. The
woman who marries him must give herself up

entirely to him, she must have no thought, no feeling besides him. But that I cannot do! I want to live for myself too! Besides, he is so nervous, so exacting. It is as if he wanted to absorb me entirely; I never feel free in his presence.'

Aniuta said all this, partly to her sister, partly to explain the fact to herself. Tania seemed to understand her and sympathise with her, but in her own heart she thought: 'What bliss it would be to live with him always, to do everything for him! how *can* Aniuta refuse such happiness?' But anyhow, Tania went to sleep that night much less unhappy than on the preceding night.

The day of departure was approaching. Fedor Michajlovitsch came once more; it was his farewell visit. He did not stay long, but his manner towards Aniuta was friendly and natural, and they promised to write to one another.

He was very affectionate with Tania, and gave her a kiss, but of course he was far from having any idea of what she had suffered for his sake.

About six months later, Aniuta received a letter from Dostojevsky telling her that he had found a wonderful young girl with whom he had fallen in love, and who had promised to marry him. This young girl was Anna Grigorjevna, his second wife. ' If anybody had told me that six months ago,' Dostojevsky added quite simply at the end of his letter, ' I give you my word of honour I should not have believed it.'

Tania's wound healed by and by. The home-journey, indeed, effaced the last trace of the storm that had raged in her heart.

The two sisters never alluded to the past event. Their sisterly affection was soon entirely restored.

They came back to Palibino, to their calm monotonous country life, but they both felt that a change *must* come soon, that great events were at hand. They seemed to be aware that they had been allowed to cast a glance into the future, and they felt convinced that something new, unusual, and important would happen in their lives. Both were seized with an immense indescribable hope, as if the years to come must bring fulfilment of all their wonderful golden dreams.

Printed by T. and A. CONSTABLE, Printers to Her Majesty, at the Edinburgh University Press.